NOTHING IS THE NUMBER WHEN YOU DIE

Also by Joan Fleming

WHEN I GROW RICH

YOUNG MAN, I THINK YOU'RE DYING

A NURI BEY MYSTERY

NOTHING IS THE NUMBER WHEN YOU DIE

JOAN FLEMING

DOVER PUBLICATIONS, INC.
Mineola, New York

Copyright

Bibliographical Note

This Dover edition, first published in 2019, is an unabridged republication of the work originally published under the imprint Collins Crime Club by William Collins, Sons, United Kingdom, in 1965.

Library of Congress Cataloging-in-Publication Data

Names: Fleming, Joan, 1908-1980, author.
Title: Nothing is the number when you die : a Nuri Bey mystery / Joan Fleming.
Description: Mineola, New York : Dover Publications, Inc., 2019. | "This Dover edition, first published in 2019, is an unabridged republication of the work originally published under the imprint Collins Crime Club by William Collins, Sons, United Kingdom, in 1965."
Identifiers: LCCN 2018040993| ISBN 9780486825687 | ISBN 048682568X
Subjects: LCSH: Philosophers—Fiction. | Turkey—Fiction.
Classification: LCC PR6011.L46 N68 2019 | DDC 823/.914—dc23
LC record available at https://lccn.loc.gov/2018040993

Manufactured in the United States by LSC Communications
82568X01 2019
www.doverpublications.com

BLACK is the colour,
SILENCE is the sound,
NOTHING is the number when you die

By Greg Stephens from the
Oxford University Experimental Theatre Club's
Hang Down Your Head and Die
first played at the Playhouse, Oxford
February 1964

Contents

PART ONE

That was Landrake

1

". . . and I shall always remember you saying, my dear Nuri, after that historic occasion, only two years ago, when your house was burnt down and all your books destroyed, that now you would study, not books, but the people amongst whom you lived."

Landrake switched on the engine of the Mini car into which he fitted so perfectly, and Nuri bey pulled his long legs inside, slammed the door and looked in surprise at his two knees towering in front of him. Though it was by no means the first time he had travelled in his friend's car, he could never accustom himself to the position in which he found himself.

"Um?" Landrake looked at him quizzically, turning his head slightly.

"You consider I made an idle boast, to study people rather than books?"

"Well, I only asked . . . as they say . . . what you think of the mutual friends we are just going to visit."

"I have known my friends Tamara and Torgüt Yenish for as many years as they have been married, even more."

Landrake drove the car slowly away from Nuri bey's frontage. "You are the most likeable of men and that is probably why you have so many friends. You are uncritical, you accept people as you find them. You are loyalty itself."

"But alas! I have made no progress in the study of people."

"You lack curiosity, that's why. You studied books because you wished to improve your knowledge but you have no wish to improve your knowledge of people. You like them or you don't like them, and that's that."

"It is possible," Nuri bey returned, stung slightly but still prepared reasonably to discuss the matter, "that I know more about my friends Yenish than you. You have known them a few years only."

"Then tell me, Nuri, what you know about them."

They came to a standstill at a traffic block in Taksim Square.

"Certainly," Nuri bey said comfortably. "Tamara is the daughter of a Russian nobleman who married an English governess of good family."

"Yes?"

"Tamara's father, fearing the Revolution, sent his young wife and baby girl to a summer residence in the Crimea, together with all the portable family heirlooms in the way of jewels, small decorative boxes of great value, *objets de virtue* . . ."

"And when she heard that their house had been ransacked and her husband killed, she fled across the Black Sea with her child and took refuge in Istanbul, carrying his fortune in a bundle. Yes, everybody knows that."

"When *I* first met Tamara, I was the same age, I a schoolboy and she a schoolgirl at the English Girls' High School, a stone's throw from here," Nuri bey leaned forward and pointed in the direction of the High School.

"And Torgüt Yenish?"

"He, a businessman, a tanner, married the girl when she was barely out of High School."

"And is the marriage a success?"

Nuri bey shrugged his shoulders at the absurdity of such a question.

Landrake smiled. "You have never asked yourself, have you? The question of whether a marriage is a success or not is not one which would enter the mind of a Turk or any other Moslem."

"Moslem! It has nothing to do with religion and anyway, I am neither a Moslem nor a Christian nor a Buddhist, as I have said many times, but something of all three. A marriage is a marriage and one would as soon ask if one's birth was a success as to ask the same question of a marriage."

Landrake laughed delightedly.

"Why are you laughing?" Nuri bey asked stiffly.

"Because East is East and West is West and however 'Westernised' you all try to get you'll never make it mentally. Forgive me, Nuri my friend, I sound damned patronising but believe me, I'm glad of this fundamental difference between us and I am quite prepared to believe your way is the better."

Nuri bey stayed quiet for some minutes whilst they drove down the Istiklal Caddesi, crowded with people who walked along the edges of the road as though there were no traffic and had to be warned by much horn-blowing. To avoid the crowds at the Galata Bridge they turned at the Galata Tower and were soon crossing the Golden Horn by the new Atatürk Bridge and driving round the outskirts of the old town of Stambul.

"What do you mean by 'an unsuccessful marriage'?" he asked at last.

"That is a question that would take a whole day to answer," Landrake returned, "but to put it in a nutshell I would say it is a marriage where the two partners do not like each other."

"You mean *love*."

"I said *like*."

"Now you are becoming absurd," Nuri bey argued. "As I see it you are trying to tell me something. Put it, please, into plain English."

"If you had a telephone, Nuri bey, I might never have entered into this conversation at all."

"It has cost me much money to build my new house. A small wooden affair though it is, much smaller than my old house, it has cost almost all I possess. I cannot at the moment afford a telephone; in fact, I do not see how I can ever have one."

"And so Tamara and Torgüt have asked me to come for you because they wish to see you. I know they want you to help them in some way and I must say I am madly curious to know how you are going to take it, Nuri bey."

Landrake was Nuri bey's British Council friend. When he was twenty-six, his young wife had died, it was said, in child-birth, now in his forties he was much in demand socially but seemed content with his bachelor existence, a friend of everyone and intimate with no one; his emotional life seemed always to take place at second-hand. He was a great gossip.

"It will be something to do with Torgüt's marvellous books," Nuri bey said comfortably. "And anything that I can do for him in that direction will be a great pleasure. Now that I have no longer any library of my own, my happiest moments are those when I can busy myself with the books of my friends."

They passed through the great gateway in the old Byzantine Walls and turned left off the Attatürk Boulevard down towards the shimmering Sea of Marmara.

The Yenish house stood facing the sea in a small, sparse garden. It was recently built with a flat roof upon which a small observatory had been erected for the apparatus of Tamara, who was a keen astrologist. A marvellous view was visible from the roof top; Seraglio Point with much of the old City of Stambul, some of Pera on the other side of the Golden Horn, with domes and minarets and the Observatory from which, even now, the date of Ramadan, the Moslem fasting period, is worked out by the stars.

Yenish was in his first floor library and received his guests with Ottoman courtesy. The Ottoman is not purely Turkish but has Persian, Greek, Armenian, Georgian and Circassian blood; the fat Turk with the sad bruised eyes occurs possibly not more than one in five. Torgüt Yenish was not more than forty-six but slim and bent as though ashamed of standing up straight and gazing ahead; his eyes were deep-set in brown caverns and his face had a great darkness.

Small glasses of coffee, on a tripod-swinging tray to avoid spilling, were brought in by a maid and the three men sat on low backless stools, only one degree removed from sitting on the floor, by the long windows open to the Sea of Marmara.

He is a man who keeps himself in secret, Nuri bey thought; he has a dark, mysterious self which he guards carefully and which I, for one, have never seen. Landrake is right, I am a shallow man, a person of poor perception, one who accepts superficial facts as the truth, and worthy to be called a scholar of books only.

Yenish and Landrake smoked and when the coffee was finished the host stated with startling directness, the object of the meeting. He now spoke Turkish.

"I want you, Nuri, my friend, to find my son Jason for me." Jason was a hero of antiquity with an extremely complicated history; a prince, resembling Hamlet in that his father's Kingdom was usurped by his uncle, but unlike Hamlet in that his uncle sent him to be brought up by a centaur, half man, half horse. He got his Kingdom back with the help of a woman much older than himself whom he married but finally abandoned for An Other. He died "*of love, of honour and of joy bereft.*" Anyone calling their child by that name might risk his being unlucky but so far Jason had turned out a youth of good looks and talent, had won a place for himself at Oxford University, England, and was reported to be doing well. Until now.

His father has heard nothing of him since he left home to return to Oxford for the Michaelmas term; he had not returned for the Christmas holidays and, now the Easter term had started, there was no word from the son.

The fanatical personal pride of the father would not allow him to write to the University authorities nor to the bank in England into which the money for the boy's keep was paid, to ask for information. In desperation the father appealed to Nuri bey. His expenses for the whole journey would, of course, be paid in full and in addition he would be pleased to give Nuri bey a reasonable sum of money.

"You are a proud man, Nuri, and you do not accept money easily. I know, however, that you can make good use of it and, if you will go and find out what has happened to my son, you will have indeed earned what I shall give you."

Landrake was not a good linguist; he could not speak Turkish fluently but he could understand everything that was said. His face wore an inscrutable expression as Yenish talked but Nuri bey thought he knew what was going on in Landrake's mind. He said:

"But why not ask someone who is familiar with England and the English way of life? I have never been out of my country and, though there was a time when I would give much to travel, and particularly to Oxford, that wish was wiped from my mind two years ago. Abroad I should cut a poor figure."

Unflatteringly, Yenish agreed but went on to say that a Turk who had never left his country, visiting Oxford for the first time and looking up the son of an old friend would bring less suspicion upon himself than, say, "our friend Landrake here."

"And besides," Landrake said in English, "I'm not due for any leave for some time. I couldn't go."

Nuri bey stared out across the smooth, silken sea to the Princes' Isles, misty on the horizon.

"Say what is in your mind, my friend," Yenish said sharply.

"Your son is no longer a child," Nuri bey replied. "There is a time when the bird leaves its nest; the father who seeks to follow him into the world outside is foolish. I cannot believe that you wish me to go, like an old woman, hurrying after him."

Landrake sniggered slightly. "A nanny," he murmured.

Yenish wrapped himself in a mysterious Eastern aura. "I have a premonition," he said hollowly, "that all is not well."

For five hundred years the Turks have clung tenaciously to the scrag end of Europe but, however much they may consider themselves Europeanised, the Western way of life lies upon them only superficially. Underneath they are unchanged and, though they will assure you that their outlook on women and marriage is the same as the Western one, this is a distinctly arbitrary statement. Though the women may show their legs and faces, go to University, run businesses, drive cars, they still, deep in the being of every Turkish male, belong to the *harem*. And still the *selamlik*, or male reception room, is inviolate and women do not settle in it as a matter of course. Nuri bey, however, felt strongly that the mother of the missing boy should be present during the discussion but no mention was made of her.

He brought up all the objections to Yenish's request that he could imagine; Yenish remained darkly imperturbable.

"I wish you to go, my friend. He is my only son and the light of my life."

"Why not go yourself?" Landrake put in.

"Impossible," Yenish replied dreamily. "Out of the question."

Nuri bey felt irritated and somehow belittled. He had on many occasions escorted V.I.P.s around Istanbul or into darkest Turkey in Asia at the request of the British Council, for a fee, but that did not mean that he was the Turkish equivalent of a kind of Universal Aunt, ready to nip about on any sort of errand for all and sundry. He remembered only too clearly and with a deep pang of emotion, all that had arisen as the result of the last errand he had carried out for a friend, starting with a simple visit to the airport and ending with drowning, murder and hanging in the square in front of the Sultan Ahmed mosque. He shuddered because he was a man of peace and wished only to be left to study philosophy, not now his own books, but those in the University and libraries of the old town.

"I cannot leave the country," Yenish murmured, "my business is entirely in my own hands, there is nobody to whom I could pass on the responsibility. My business is *me* and if I am not here there will be no money to come back to and I must remind you, my friend, that it costs me a great deal of money to send my son to England to the University of Oxford. The air fares alone . . . I am not a rich man."

But not a poor one, Nuri bey mused, looking round. He had by now decided not to go but it would have shown lack of courtesy and friendship to make a definite statement at present.

"Allow me," he said at last, "allow me to think over your proposition."

"Nuri, my friend, I beg of you to make a swift decision, every hour that passes may be vital to my son's safety."

Nuri bey stood up. "Torgüt, I fear you are withholding some information, you do not seem to be telling me the whole story. Why should your son be in any danger?"

He did not expect a straight answer and he did not get one. His host writhed with circumlocution, his mind and body distorted in the effort to give a simple answer to a question requiring an extremely complicated reply. He was a devious and circuitous man.

Nuri bey moved towards the door. "There is always the boy's mother, she might go," he murmured. Landrake, rising also, gave a sudden and inexplicable bark of laughter. Yenish was at once angry though he made some effort to conceal it. He rose to usher his guests out.

"You refuse to take me seriously," he snapped, tight-lipped. "This may be a matter of life and death."

Nuri bey stopped. "Why?" he said. "Why? Why?"

"I should have to have your assurance that you would go before I told you any more. Furthermore, I should tell you in the strictest confidence," the Turk replied, "and not," his dark glance raked the Englishman, "*not* before any foreigners." Landrake, hands deep in his pockets, remained unruffled; he smiled good-humouredly.

"You took me into your confidence in asking me to fetch Nuri bey to your house," he said lightly.

Yenish continued to stare angrily at Landrake. "It was you who suggested Nuri to go on this journey for me. You have judged our friend wrongly. He is not willing to go. He smells danger," he sneered.

Nuri bey clenched his hands; he was slow to anger but when he was angry it resembled a searing wind which, blowing down in icy fury from the Arctic, scorches everything in its path. He did not wish to have his temper roused. He looked at the bookshelves built round his friend's library, an unrewarding sight because all the books were arranged on the shelves backwards so that the page-edges faced the room and the titles were written on little sticky paper labels stuck flat on the shelf in front of each book. It gave a curiously untidy, even mad, appearance to the room.

"I sould like to talk to Tamara," he said tightly.

"Tamara is in her room; she is greatly distressed by the present circumstances; she has no wish to see anyone."

"Then I will take leave of you," Nuri bey said courteously, "and go home to think over the problem."

A gleam came into Yenish's sunken eyes. "Then all hope is not fled?"

"Good old Nuri!" Landrake exclaimed schoolboyishly. "That's the stuff!"

"Farewell," Nuri bey said stiffly. "There is no need for you to take me home, I should prefer to walk as I have much to think about."

2

It was a long walk back through Samatya, keeping to the sea road and, as he walked, Nuri bey thought a number of depressing thoughts. What am I? Who am I? What have I done in life? What does life hold for me? Why do I, in fact, go on living? Always my problems are those of other people. I have many friends and they are important to me but are my friends my life? I should have married, Nuri bey thought. To wait for love is fatal. After my mother died, I should have married the first woman to whom I was attracted. If I had done so, I would not now be for ever observing life at a distance.

And as he walked, his thoughts became less general and more particular. I could have married Tamara when we were both seventeen. She was as beautiful as the moon. Her son would also have been my son and with what pleasure I would have flown to England to rescue him from the clutches of some unsuitable female! Only he would not have been named Jason but some grand name like Omar, or perhaps some fine-sounding British name like Pendennis.

The Persians often compare women to the moon, there is no higher compliment than for a woman to be "beautiful as the moon." But, in fact, Nuri bey mused, there was a certain moonlight quality about the half-Russian, half-English Tamara. He remembered now how distressed he had been when this beautiful moonlight-coloured girl of seventeen had married the dark (though it must be admitted, handsome) Yenish whom she hardly knew. Marriage to a near-stranger is a commonplace in Turkey but Tamara, with her ash-blonde hair, her silvery-pale face and her light grey eyes with their fantastically long lashes, was physically as far removed as anyone could be from the man she married. Nuri bey considered it had been somewhat of a *mésalliance*; Jason, their only son, was good-looking enough but there had been no more children after the first.

When his thoughts reached their lowest ebb, he decided that he needed food and went into a small café, a mere hole in the wall near the University. There he ate chicken and aubergine covered with a delicious cheese sauce and served piping hot in a small earthenware dish. He met a bookseller friend with whom he had a long discussion about a book which had come into the bookseller's hands called *City of God*, a best-seller, whose author, St. Augustine, never received a royalty in his life. The discussion was a pleasurable one; Nuri forgot his gloomy introspection and enjoyed himself, sipping scalding hot tea and sitting in the mild sun in the dirty courtyard at the back of the café with his friend. But when a stray cat had sent a shower of dirt off a low-hanging roof into his glass of tea and the sun had moved round, it was time to go. Nuri bey walked down through the covered market to the Galata Bridge, crossed it slowly, and swung on to a tram that rattled up the hill through busy Pera towards his home.

It was four and a half hours since he had left home. As Nuri bey put his key in the lock a small boy arrived on a bicycle, handing him an envelope. On being asked who he was, he said he was the son of the chauffeur of Torgüt Yenish and had been sent with the note by the lady of the house. He looked with troubled eyes at Nuri bey as he pocketed the coin given him and departed. A letter from Tamara, Nuri bey started; he had never received a letter from Tamara and, in view of the thoughts which he had been thinking as he walked home from the Yenish house, it was a shock to receive one now. He fingered it thoughtfully. He had no doubt as to what it contained. Tamara wished to add her persuasions to those of her husband. He was trapped. If Tamara asked him to go to England to rescue her son from whatever may have befallen him, then he would have to go. For Tamara, he thought fulsomely, he would go to the planet Mars. He sat dreamily staring down at the note, still unopened.

He heard a car stop outside, someone banged on the door; still holding the note he went to open it. Landrake stood outside.

"Come in," Nuri bey began, courteously as ever.

"He is dead," Landrake said unemotionally.

"You mean . . . Yenish?"

Landrake nodded.

"How do you know?"

"They telephoned to me at the British Council; my secretary rang through to my flat; I had just arrived home."

"Who telephoned?"

"Tamara asked her chauffeur to telephone me."

Nuri bey tore open the envelope:

Dear Nuri,

Torgüt has been found shot dead in his library. Can you come at once, I am in great distress.

Yours,
Tamara

He passed it to Landrake.

"But it is all so quick," he said.

"These things are quick. Quick and clean."

"I can't believe it," Nuri bey said.

"Oh, I can," Landrake said fervently. "He was a frightened man, couldn't you see that?"

"Frightened of what?"

"Frightened . . .!"

"But Yenish was the most respectable of citizens," Nuri argued. "He has many friends in the city; he is well known both in Istanbul and Pera. We had much in common with our book collections. Landrake, could it possibly be that my refusal to go to England for him drove him to shooting himself?"

"Of course not. You left the door open, as it were; you said you'd think it over." There was a pause. "Throughout history you Turks have been great murderers," Landrake said, pacing up and down the hall, "but since your revolution you seem only to murder for a cause. Now, you are great *assassins*, you assassinate right, left and centre; the word itself is your very own, it comes from the Arabic *hashshash*, dating from the Crusades when your old sheik, Old Man of the Mountains, sent out his Moslem fanatics to kill the Christian leaders. They filled themselves with *hashish* to get themselves in the right mood. Don't you know your history?" He stopped his flippant discourse short. Nuri bey's mouth was a small tight line, his eyes mere boot buttons.

"Murder? Was he *murdered*?"

Landrake took his bunch of keys from his pocket and, tossing them casually, he turned away towards the window.

"I said assassinated."

"You mean . . . he did not die by his own hand?"

"The message I got from my secretary," Landrake said, turning round, "was that Yenish has been found shot dead. I took it to mean that he was shot by someone because suicide seems so unlikely."

"So does murder!" Nuri bey said, "so does murder!"

But driving down through Pera, along the route which they had taken what seemed a long time previously but was in fact so recent, he speculated on the possibility of suicide. Yenish was a melancholy man; it might be that his son's disappearance had weighed upon his mind and that Nuri bey's apparent unwillingness to go and look for him had tipped the balance and he had shot himself on impulse.

"We'll soon see," Landrake said.

"What did he say after I had gone?"

"Man! I left almost at the same time. You whizzed off like a scalded cat."

"But did he say anything about me?"

"He thanked me for bringing you and asked me if I thought you would go."

"And what did you say?"

"Something like, his guess was as good as mine. I wished him luck. Then I left; I passed you on the road; didn't you see me?"

"No; I walked back along the sea-front."

At the Yenish villa all was chaos. There was nothing to stop the two friends entering and walking upstairs to the big room overlooking the sea where they had been entertained so recently. The body lay across one of the low stools upon which they had sat; the tray of tiny coffee glasses was upset, the remains of the sweetmeat strewn across the carpet. The body was now covered with a piece of antique silken brocade and the three servants were being questioned. In the few minutes Nuri bey and Landrake stood listening in the background several facts emerged out of the confusion of shouting, talking, weeping, accusation and counter-accusation: Yenish had been shot three times, through the head, the chest and the stomach; no gun had yet been found. The two maids had heard the shots, they had been in the wash-house tidying up; the gardener had, contrary to all rules, been in the washhouse with them; the sound of the shot had been heard by all three but apparently they had been making so much noise themselves that they were confused as to where the shots had come from. In other words, the three had been having fun—Turkish. The chauffeur lived with his wife and family in a hut some distance away; he had been out in the car, filling up with gasoline and had returned to take his master to his office. It was he who had found the body, it would seem not more than a few minutes after death.

It was said that Madame had been sleeping; tired after a late night, she had taken a sleeping pill; after finding the body, the chauffeur had banged loudly upon her door and, hearing no response, had sent the maids in to wake her. She had taken a few moments to rouse. She was said to have heard nothing and the sound of the shots had not wakened her.

When the police at last got round to Nuri bey and Landrake, they were asked for their part in the events. Nuri bey said that he had said good-bye to his two friends in the library, had left the house to walk back to Istanbul along the sea-road, had had a meal at a restaurant near the University and had arrived home to find a boy with a note awaiting him. He had known Yenish bey many years, they were good friends.

Landrake, too, had been a friend of Yenish bey for many years; he and Nuri bey here had been visiting Yenish bey this morning as they had done very often. Nothing unusual had occurred, Yenish bey had seemed his normal self. He had left the house more or less at the same time as Nuri bey, had driven back into Istanbul where he had lunched at Pandoli's restaurant. (They would confirm this as he was well-known there.) Later he and an American journalist friend, eating at the same restaurant, had gone together for drinks at the Park Hotel; they had sat in the bar there for some time. Later still Landrake had seen his friend off in an airport bus at the terminus and had gone to buy himself some new pocket handkerchiefs in the Istiklal Caddesi. He had returned to his flat to receive the shocking news of Yenish bey's death from his secretary, on the telephone. All this was taken down laboriously in a notebook by one of the police officers, translated into Turkish by Nuri bey.

"I've got to get back to the office," Landrake said when the interrogation was over and Nuri bey went to the front door with him. "Doesn't Tamara want to see you? You'd better stay."

"She seems in no great hurry," Nuri bey returned dryly. "I think she will want to say that now this has happened, it is absolutely necessary that I go to England. Someone will have to find the boy to tell him that his father is dead."

Landrake stared thoughtfully at Nuri bey whilst taking a cigarette out and lighting it.

"Well, how do you feel about it now?"

"Less inclined than before. If I had consented I feel sure Yenish would have had more to tell me, something to, as you would say, *go on.* As it is . . ." he shrugged expressively. "What do I go forth for to seek, and what manner of thing do I expect to find?"

With that maddening retreat into flippancy that one met with so often in Landrake, he said, "It's up to you, friend."

"It's not like that," Nuri bey said irritably. "If, by going, I shall do good, okay, as you would say. But if I find the boy and for some reason he is not willing to come home, what good will it do? It would only make his mother more unhappy than before."

"I can't help you. It's something you must decide for yourself."

Nuri bey nodded absently and turned back into the house. Landrake started the engine but Nuri bey swung back and leaned down to speak to him through the window. "You told them, upstairs, that nothing unusual happened this morning and that Yenish seemed his usual self. Was that wise? It was not true."

Landrake switched off the engine and, taking his cigarette out of his mouth, he turned it round and round, examining the end. "I thought it best. No good starting up something by mentioning family affairs. Might make matters a whole lot worse. I should say that, without a doubt, the line they'll take up over this thing is that it's a political murder; they go on happening all the time and most of them get hushed up. They'll keep this out of the papers, they'll hush it up and our poor friend will be hustled off into the arms of Allah, we hope, with the greatest possible speed and least possible fuss. You'll see. I'd keep your trap shut about the missing boy if I were you."

Nuri bey nodded. "I'm afraid you're right, my friend. I do not interest myself in politics; it is too dangerous."

"Quite!" With a cryptic twist of his mouth and a spurt of gravel across the knees of Nuri bey's best brown pinstriped suit, Landrake disappeared.

She *was* as beautiful as the moon, still, some twenty years after Nuri bey had first realised it. There was nothing about her face or features which resembled that satellite but the light with which she shone, and her colouring. To add to the illusion, she was wearing a silver-blue negligée and her hair, usually piled neatly on top of her small head, was in disarray, falling down behind in long fronds of unearthly delicacy of substance. Her eyes were the strange colour of a goat's eyes, pale grey and yellow, the irises opening and closing with the sensitivity of those of a cat so that you had to watch them all the time in case you missed something. They were now quite tearless but hardly any iris showed, only huge black pupils.

". . . and I have always known, perhaps I have wished, that one day he would die."

It took Nuri bey's breath away.

"I have never guessed that he was so deeply involved politically," he murmured.

"Oh, let's leave it like that, then. There is no point in implicating you in all my troubles, any more than I need. But in one thing I was in complete agreement with my husband, and that was in asking you to go and look for Jason. When he told me that Landrake had suggested asking you I was so pleased." She came across and touched his arm.

"I did not agree to do so when Torgüt asked me this morning."

She gasped slightly and drew back.

"I left saying that I would think it over."

She swallowed and he watched the rise and fall of her beautiful white throat.

"Tamara," he said, "for the love of Allah, do not approach me; even in moments of great tragedy such as we are experiencing now, a man is still a man and not a eunuch."

She moved away and Nuri bey sat down on a low seat, folded his arms and stared at her mandarin-like, unsmiling.

"Nuri bey," she said very distinctly, "will you go to England to look for my son?"

"I must know more about it before I say yes."

"I have nothing to tell you that could help. I only know that Jason greatly enjoyed his holiday at home last year. We bought him a small sailing boat, he had a friend from Oxford to stay and they were out all day, having what the friend called a 'wonderful time.' The boat is now over at Moda Yacht Club and has been there the whole autumn."

"He had Turkish friends, too, I gather?"

"Certainly, old school friends, people he met at the Yacht Club."

"There must be some connection, Tamara, between what happened here to-day and the silence of Jason, no?"

"Torgüt was involved politically. He had strong feelings about the Government, he may have been in some counter-Government scheme. I do not know."

"And Jason. These young students are the ones who start the revolutions, hot-headed, opinionated beyond their years."

"But Jason was not like that, he had no interest in Turkish politics. He has spent two years at Oxford and is now in his final year. During the long vacation both last year and the year before he went to England, he travelled in America and South America and all over Europe. He has never been home long enough since he grew up to involve himself in our politics, such as they are." She sprang up and walked about the room, wringing her hands. "Nuri bey, if you must know, Torgüt was a dark and solitary man, for all he seemed to have many friends. For many years he and I have lived as strangers in this house. I didn't begin to understand him and if I had had a strong enough character, I should have left him." She stopped in front of him. "I did not have the courage, and that is the truth. I have had my son and I still have my stars; what Torgüt did was of no interest to me and I don't honestly care who killed Torgüt, or why. He is dead and I thank God for it."

Nuri bey felt a cold shiver run down his spine. Tamara's English mother had never been able to speak Russian, nor had she ever learned much Turkish after her escape to Constantinople. Consequently Tamara had been brought up speaking English, Russian and Turkish. The words which she now spoke were English and so foreign to anything a Turkish woman would say that Nuri bey was scared while at the same time feeling a kind of dread admiration. Direct speech, especially from a woman, was unknown to him.

There was a long pause, the pupils of Tamara's eyes were still enormous. Then: "Jason must come home, otherwise he may not receive his patrimony. All Torgüt's property will be his but he must be here to prove that he still lives, otherwise there will be endless complications."

"But what about you?"

"Moneywise, you mean?" Again she jumped up nervously. "I'm all right," she said. "I wouldn't touch a lira of Torgüt's money and the sooner I am out of this house the better."

"But how will you live?"

"In the last resort I can always cast horoscopes," she smiled. "But first, I must find a place where I can have my telescope and things."

"But Tamara . . ."

"Oh . . . don't worry, Nuri bey, my dear mother was a prudent North-country woman. That bundle she brought away from Russia contained a lot more than her baby's nappies. The Russians literally hung themselves with jewels in those affluent days before the Revolution, and when they were so loaded that they could hardly walk, they carried in their hands utterly useless, but priceless things, like diamond and enamel bouquets. There was one emerald and diamond parure the sale of which kept my mother and me quite comfortably in that small flat we had until I went to school. She was able to buy an annuity for herself here in Turkey, and one for me, and she sent most of the rest of the treasure to London, not long before she died. An old schoolteacher friend took them in her suitcase and deposited them in a vault in the City of London. So you see, I can give you the key to that safe deposit and you can take out a piece of jewellery and sell it at a sale room in Bond Street and you would have a lump sum, if you should need it in your search for Jason."

They sat silently for a few moments and suddenly she shuddered violently. "'*Money withers,*' he used to say solemnly, '*and is gone. We must not serve money, but Allah!*' Ugh! He was such an appalling hypocrite. He served no god but *money, money, money*. He will have left a small fortune, you'll see."

"Only this morning," Nuri bey said firmly, "he told us he was not a rich man."

Tamara looked down at her twisting, flawless white hands. "Poor me," she said, "pity me, Nuri my dear."

Nuri my dear: how pleasant it was! He had so often been called *Nuri my lion*. He liked *Nuri my dear* a lot better.

"A highly-strung, fatherless girl, half-Russian, half-English, living on soil that was foreign to both parents, growing up amongst expatriates and seventeen when the Second World War blew up. I fell for Torgüt in a school-girlish way; I had a crush on him. My mother thought that here was security for me at last; she encouraged me. We married and I . . . I grew up. I found myself the *thing*, the absolute possession of a dark-hearted, self-contained, self-absorbed, killingly-mean man whose language I could not master. That's how it was and that's how it comes about that I can't shed a tear, not one single tear, to-day. Give me a cigarette."

He did not give her a cigarette. He did something else, he wrapped his arms round her and drew her towards him and kissed her passionately. It was a staggering and completely unbelievable thing, but it was happening. His arms felt so long that they seemed to go round and round her, though she was by no means slim; he felt terribly tall, a king, a conqueror, a man to end all men, the first man and the last man, the *only* man. He raised his head from her face and gave a great shout of delight and at once bent his head to its business.

3

Sylvia was Landrake's small cabin cruiser, the pride of his life. He had bought it, as he said, to "comfort his sad heart" when his mother died, with a sum of money she had left him and it had, indeed, fully served that purpose. He kept her in a boat house on the Golden Horn where, during the winter, she was painted and varnished and polished and maintained by her owner as no boat has ever been looked after. After Ramadan, when the weather began to be charming, he would take her proudly down, under the Galata Bridge.

The waters of the Bosphorus are tricky because four great Russian rivers run into the Black Sea from which the only outlet is the Bosphorus, an eighteen mile long crack between Asia and Europe down which this great mass of water rushes as though it were, as someone said, being pulled through a keyhole. In places it is not as wide as the Thames at Woolwich. By the Leander Tower, opposite the Golden Horn, which is at the Southern limit, the tides of the Sea of Marmara, with the Ægean pushing along behind, try to thrust their way up the Bosphorus and the resulting underwater confusion is such that no submarine has yet dared to travel below water to the Black Sea.

It looks so comparatively peaceful and lake-like on the surface on a sunny, calm day; rowing boats skim along and dozens of small steamers ply across and across. Landrake prided himself on his "Bosmanship" as he called it and on the day after Yenish's death he called for Nuri bey with the suggestion that they "make themselves scarce for a couple of days."

"We haven't been asked to stick around," he said, "we've given them all the information we possibly can . . . I say, what's happened? You look pretty pleased with yourself?"

"I am satisfied," Nuri bey said smugly, "because I have made up my mind."

"Oh, what to do?"

"Several things. The first is to go to England to search for Jason."

"You are? When are you going?"

"When the stars are propitious," he returned loftily. "That is, probably one day this week. To-day I can spend with you, to-morrow I must return to make my arrangements, though fortunately I have my passport."

Landrake laughed; he had always been amused by Nuri bey's pride in the passport which so far had never been used. "At last it's coming in useful; well done!"

Armed with a large pair of extraordinarily powerful field-glasses, Landrake steered his little craft up the left bank of the Bosphorus. Now and then he would hold the wheel with one hand and raise the glasses, looking through them with alert attention at every vessel that passed. At Büyükdere they stopped for lunch at a fish restaurant at the water's edge from the windows of which the opening into the Black Sea was clearly visible.

Landrake drank a Thracian white wine and Nuri bey drank Coca-Cola and whisky for, though the Prophet forbids the drinking of wine by his followers, he said nothing about the drinking of spirits, which had not been invented in his day. In any case, Nuri bey much preferred spirits.

"Tell me what happened yesterday," Landrake said. "I mean when you saw Tamara."

Nuri bey smiled, there were certain things he could never tell. Landrake looked at him curiously. "Well, go on. How did she persuade you to say you'd go to England?"

But Nuri bey was not telling. Instead he said that the conversation they had had in the car yesterday when driving down in the morning to see Yenish had been oddly prophetic, they had talked about marriage, about unsuccessful marriage about *love* and *like*. Landrake was right; it was important that one should take these things into consideration. He had considered the situation and, if he had not done so, he might have been disturbed that Tamara was not the brokenhearted wife. She had, in fact, taken the whole thing calmly but it was not surprising when one could guess at the truth.

"That they hated each other?"

"Too strong a word; they were indifferent."

"I'm glad you don't think she shot him," Landrake said blandly, helping himself to another glass of wine.

Nuri bey felt slightly winded. "Oh, no, I did not think that," he murmured hurriedly. "Did you?"

Landrake thoughtfully picked his teeth. "Could be."

"After you had gone? No, no. Nothing like it. As it is, my friend, we too are lucky to be above suspicion."

"But are we? And Tamara's revolver stayed in her drawer, wrapped in a silk petticoat?"

"Has she a gun?" Nuri bey asked, again keeping calm.

"Yes, indeed. Four years ago she asked me to buy her an automatic in London. It was when things were very bad out here politically; feelings were running high, she was scared when she was alone in the house. I showed her how to work it; we drove out into the woods up behind here once or twice in her car and she fired into an old sack under my supervision. It is just as well, you know, on the edge of a civil war it might be useful."

"We must be thankful that the question of her gun had not arisen."

But in addition to his elation, Nuri bey to-day felt more than usually thoughtful, impressed by how much one may not know about friends whom one has had for years.

Back on board the boat, Nuri bey took the wheel; there were few active pleasures he enjoyed more: to sit up on the pilot's stool sheltered by the windscreen, the sun warm through one's shirt, sleeves rolled up, hands on the wheel which answered to the slightest touch, the soft regular sound from the exhausts and the hissing of the water as it parted before the sharp demand of the prow, gave him extreme pleasure.

It was choppy as they left the Bosphorus and entered the dark waters of the Black Sea, turning Eastwards and chugging quietly along the coast-line whilst Landrake kept his huge field-glasses up to his eyes. To-day, Nuri bey thought as he watched his friend, to-day all their actions seemed charged with significance, as though at a beginning . . . or an end. He had often seen his friend scanning the coastline with the same attention but to-day: "Some day you will see the fabulous bird for which you seek," he said lightly.

"*Wheresoever the carcase is, there will be the eagles gathered together.*"

"Eagles! We have no eagles here."

Landrake laughed and, putting down his glasses, stood behind the windscreen and lighted a cigarette beside Nuri bey, looking across the cabin roof at the calm sea and misty land ahead.

"I have seen the eagles," Landrake said mysteriously, "it is the carcase that I now seek. I am speaking in parables, my friend: a quotation from our Bible which, with all your reading, you should know. The time has come to speak plainly to you, Nuri. Two years ago you behaved with great bravery. You took, in all innocence, a small case of compressed blocks of opium alkaloid, grown in Turkey and in a condition to be easily converted into heroin in back kitchens, to be sold in England or U.S.A. But you got yourself into a shocking mess from which you emerged with great credit, at the same time getting one of the worst drug-trafficking agents in this country . . . well, let's call it 'out of the way,' shall we?"

"That is all over and done with."

"Think so? It was *not* all over and done with, my friend. Nuri, I once knew a young girl of nineteen, beautiful, happy and clever. She had a job but she gave it up to marry a soldier in the Royal Engineers whom I knew well. She started to have a baby. The soldier was reported missing, the baby died at birth; the girl was mad with grief. To occupy herself she worked in a canteen for American soldiers and there she met someone who started her on drugs, first marihuana (reefers, they call it), and then on to shots of heroin. After a time the husband was reported not dead but in an army prison camp in Germany but by then it was too late, the drug habit had taken hold. When, two and a half years later, he came home at the end of the War, the lovely girl of nineteen was a shrivelled hag of twenty-three. He sent her to a home and she came out supposedly cured; she was back there . . . oh, well, no point in going into it blow by blow. It went on for years; then she died, thank God."

Nuri bey shuddered.

"To me drug-trafficking is the one and only unforgivable sin. And since your experience with that Miasma woman I have done my utmost to discover *who*, and *how* and *where*, above all *where* the plant is grown here, in Turkey. I can't tackle the far bigger problem of where it is grown in the Far East because my job happens to be here."

"And have you had any success?"

Landrake nodded. "Some," he replied. "I'm getting hot. When I do find where it is grown, there's going to be a godawful explosion, I mean literally; one great big hole in Turkey and your friend Landrake will probably disappear in a mushroom of smoke . . . into Russia, or the Caucasus, or Bulgaria, well, in any case, I don't intend to tell you where. It's just important not to run the *Sylvia* too hard up against anything." He laughed a little at Nuri bey's look of disbelief, horror and alarm. "Take care," he shouted, clutching the wheel.

Nuri bey having now clearly lost his enthusiasm for steering, Landrake nudged his friend off the stool and took the wheel into his own hands. "You are now pea-green with fright," Landrake observed cheerfully, "but that does not disturb me; only a frightened man can be a brave one, he who is not frightened cannot be brave."

Nuri bey looked his friend slowly up and down: Landrake was a small neat man with a round cheerful face which wore an habitual half-smile, and had smooth brown hair which fitted his head closely. He was always dressed suitably for the occasion and now he was wearing a silk scarf neatly but loosely tied under his white open-necked shirt. The perfect Englishman.

"You are mad," Nuri bey said, "but you English are all mad, and that has often been said before."

"Not really mad, that's the word you use to reconcile yourself to it, I suppose."

Nuri bey was quiet for a long time, watching the grey characterless coastline slipping by. He picked up the field-glasses and looked through them: farms, huts and small landing places immediately sprang into the picture. Soon Landrake made a wide sweep to starboard and they went towards the land. They were approaching what appeared to be the delta of a small river; the *Sylvia* slowed down.

"See how shallow it's getting? I can't go inland much farther. But here, Nuri bey, my friend, here we can almost smell that stinking carcase."

"And the eagles?"

"Birds of the air! They have no webbed feet. But from time to time they leave this place to fish, rowing, or in a boat with a tiny outboard motor." He switched off the engine and they rocked slowly to a stand-still. The scene was desolate, even in the sunshine; there was a distant line of low grey hills from which the river rose, but otherwise the landscape was quite featureless.

"I'm on my own," Landrake said. "It's better so, and it's taken me almost a couple of years to get so far. I don't know what this district is called, or this river. It's not much of a river, by the way."

"You've explored it inland?"

"Yes, on solitary duck-shooting expeditions with a mule. I've been up the river as far as it goes, it peters out in several small streams only about ten miles up. There's no road beyond the military zone which ends about eight miles Bosphorus-wards. It's a kind of no-man's-land. No gypsy would settle here, but what do you think? There *is* a tribe of what looks like gypsies; they fish in the delta; they shoot too . . ." Landrake gave Nuri bey a long, thoughtful look. "I'm taking you into my absolute confidence, Nuri, because time is getting short. If I disappear . . ."—he waved his hand vaguely Westwards—"then I'll be here, somewhere within three square miles of this place . . . dead or . . .?"

Nuri bey had been listening almost without drawing a breath in case he missed anything. Now emotion overcame him and he clasped Landrake's hand in both of his. "My friend," he stammered, in great agitation of mind, "my friend!"

"Not to worry," Landrake said lightly. "I'm doing what I want to do, you don't sympathise with people for that. I felt the time had come to tell someone and you're the best person I know. Before we part I'll show you whereabout the explosive is hidden and also I'm making arrangements with Hassan, where I tie up in the summer, so that you can take out the *Sylvia* alone, if necessary . . ."

"But . . ."

"Don't worry; it may not be necessary. It's only a precaution. Now, will you remember this place?" He pointed to the dials in front of him. "We were here when we started from Istanbul: memorise these figures and perhaps sometime . . ."

They stood in silence staring at the coastline; nothing moved, no figure was seen.

"Just remember, that's all," Landrake murmured as he switched on the engine, "in case I'm not here when you need to. And on this solemn note I want you to bear in mind this drug question when you go to England."

Nuri bey started.

"Don't get the wind up. We've both seen Jason often enough when he was a boy, home from school in Switzerland, and growing up. I met him often at Moda Club last summer. His mother has always spoken English to him; in fact, he has none of his father's dark looks, he's got Tamara's big Slav, sloping eyes: otherwise he talks and looks like any English undergraduate."

"I know all that. Is there not anything else you can tell me?"

"I swear, Nuri, if there were anything else about the young man and his apparent disappearance I knew that would help you, I should certainly tell you. But there isn't. And yesterday was the first time I heard that he was missing. It's probably some girl he's got entangled with, ten to one."

Across and across the surface of the Bosphorus, in bands of dozens, fleet-winged black birds skim; they are as rapidly flying as swallows. They are nameless and no one knows where they come from or where they go to. Whereas swifts scream happily round the house on summer's evenings, these birds, though they resemble swifts, make no sound at all. They are ghost-birds and, because no one has ever seen one stationary or found one dead, legend has grown up round them and many superstitious people believe that they are the restless souls of the unshriven Byzantines who were killed at the time of the Conquest, four hundred years ago. It was dusk as they slid home down the Bosphorus, lights were coming on in the *yalis* along the banks and a great flock of the birds passed them so closely that they felt the movement of their wings like a cold draught.

"I am filled with a great fear," Nuri bey said, "I have had a happy day but to-night the world seems full of an unseen enemy. I know not who is my friend and who is my enemy. I know not why Yenish died or who killed him; I am in a state of great bewilderment."

"Well, I'm your friend, and that's one thing you can be certain of. Nuri the Lion-hearted they called you after the Miasma trial: you only need something to be brave about. And I think, mind, I say *I think* . . . you'll find it."

4

Unaccountably not destroyed in the fire was Nuri bey's mother-of-pearl dustpan; with this and a red plastic hand-brush he was crawling round his living room brushing up the dust. His new house was built of wood, by his special desire, because he had always lived in wood, and it consisted of one large ground-floor room with small kitchen and bathroom adjoining, and two bedrooms on the first floor. It was sparsely furnished with a divan, two overstuffed armchairs (made in England especially for the Middle East market and indescribably ugly), of which, the Turks having only recently graduated to chairs, Nuri bey was inordinately proud. There were built-in book shelves upon which pathetically stood a small group of books given him by some of his friends. As those who had given him books were bibliophiles, and naturally mean with their possessions, the books were not of best quality, nor even second-best, but they were undoubtedly books and they leaned and lolled together, a motley lot, mere refugees. A built-in electric fire replaced the magnificent old black stove from which an enormous pipe rose and strode blackly across the ceiling of the old house. Nuri bey disliked the new heater and treated it with the formality due to a stranger. An old Caucasian rug lay in front of it, given him by Torgüt Yenish. He picked it up and shook it, sending dust flying all over the room he had just brushed, and replaced it lovingly. He had some good friends, nearly everyone he knew had contributed something to his new house and he was surrounded by tokens of their regard.

From the light in his great eyes and the lightness of movement with which he performed his tasks no one could mistake him for anyone other than a lover expecting his lady. He had arrived home at midnight after his day with Landrake to find a note from her awaiting him. The note told him that the Yenish house was full of policemen, advised him not to come near and said that she would come, driving her own small car, at the first moment in the day that she could escape without attracting undue attention.

Nuri bey still had the old carpet bag, descended from his grandfather, made at Asprey's in Bond Street, London, at the time of the Great Exhibition, and given to his grandfather by one of the Sultans for a reason lost in the mists of time. This bag and its contents had been the only possession left from the fire, with the exception of the few kitchen utensils and the mother-of-pearl dustpan and, though he was fully aware that it would look incongruous in, say, a London bus, he had no other piece of luggage. He brought it out and examined it lovingly, brushing the inside and giving a spit and polish to the metal buckles attached to the two straps which could be fastened when the case was filled to bursting point. He was not too happy about his best suit and intended to take it to the valet service in the Istiklal Caddesi at the earliest opportunity to be cleaned and pressed. His shoes too . . . but he knew of a good shoe-black near the Park Hotel; he would wear one pair and take his second pair in a parcel under his arm, changing rapidly and unobserved behind the taxi (or *dolmus*) rank. He took out his passport and studied it carefully. The outside was shabby because he always carried it with him (like the Mad Hatter who always took a plate in case he found a plum cake) but the inside was virgin, with no rubber stamp or scribble to show that he had ever been abroad.

As Landrake had given him a starting key of the *Sylvia*, so he would give Landrake one key of his house so that his friend could come in to see that all was well in Nuri bey's absence. He was so upset, so startled, so excited by the events of the past two days that he had had no time for anything more than a passing nod at himself. His travel arrangements now complete, he sat cross-legged upon his Caucasian rug and stared himself straight in the face, marvelling at what he found. A bachelor of thirty-eight, he had never been in love save, perhaps, two years ago, when he wavered on the edge of an absurd affair with an English girl of twenty. And yet, upon the instant, he found himself passionately and deeply in love with a woman he had known since he was seventeen, half Russian, half English, and this he thought the most extraordinary and wonderful thing to happen though, in fact, it was all quite simple. Though Nuri bey would deny that he was a Moslem and say, in a woolly-minded way, that he was of any and every religion, the fact was that he was a dyed-in-the-wool Moslem, imbued from birth in the Moslem way of life. His reading had taught him that women are of as much importance in the cosmic scheme as men and not mere vessels for the carrying of men, but his instinct was that women had no souls, which is Moslem belief. Thus towards any Turkish woman with whom he had made love, he had felt, if not consciously, a slight contempt, and had had no wish to make her his wife. When he saw suddenly, as though in a great flash of light, that this wonderful Russian-English moon-woman was immediately accessible and could be his for the taking, he wasted no time.

In certain conditions he could take off momentarily into an extrasensory dimension, an attribute inherited from a psychic aunt. This he now did, looking down at himself from somewhere in the air a few feet above and watching himself handling, with great expertise, the vibratingly passionate woman in his arms. The way he was behaving and the exaggeratedly emotional things he was saying would have made him blush furiously if he had had any corporate body, at the moment, with which to blush. Back inside himself, cross-legged upon the Caucasian rug, he sat upright listening like an intelligent dog, ears pricked, for the sound of his mistress's arrival.

Though by no means slim, Tamara had tiny hands and feet and delicately fragile ankles; she moved with the lightness of foot and swiftness of a young girl. To-day she was wearing the lightest of blue silk raincoats over an eggshell blue silk dress and her eyes seemed to have taken on the same unearthly pale blue.

Nuri bey was soon conducting himself exactly as he had demonstrated to himself shortly before; it was as though he had studied a blueprint for love-making.

"This is the most wonderful thing that has ever happened to me," he said, raising his face from her creamy throat. She laughed, throwing her head back and laughing into his face. He was enchanted; laughter is seldom heard in Istanbul.

"Haven't you had enough of Turkish men?" he asked soberly.

"Of one Turk, yes. But you . . . you're so tall, Nuri, you're not a typical Turk."

"What is a typical Turk? We are a mixed breed. I am tall from my mother's family, who fled from Circassia into Turkey when the

Russians occupied their country. Three hundred thousand of them had to leave and as they left the shores each one fired his gun three times." He did not add, because he did not know, that his Circassian grandfather had grown immensely tall through being breast-fed by a series of wet-nurses until he was ten, breast milk being considered an essential food for warriors.

Nuri bey took her hands in his. "There is a time for everything, and when the time comes for making love to you . . . why, we will surprise your stars." He clapped his hands together and looked at her over them.

"You mean . . . with my dead husband still above ground we should not make love? Perhaps you are right." She gave an enchanting small smile with two dimples appearing on either side of her mouth.

"Nuri . . . you must not come near our house. They have taken away the body for examination and they have left behind a great many people who have taken over the library as a kind of office. They are going through all Torgüt's private papers and making lists of all his friends and acquaintances and they are going to interview everyone. If Torgüt has left any records of anything he may be involved in politically, he will have been very, very foolish. But somehow I don't think he has. For instance . . ."—she opened her handbag and brought out several things—"here is a bundle of English money; it was in the small secret safe we have in our room for which both of us had keys. I keep my jewels in it. He had money in dollars, in pounds and some Swiss francs. This is about two hundred pounds and I am giving it to you for your fares and hotels. And this," she held up a thin gold chain with a cross heavily encrusted with pearls, amethysts and diamonds, "I should like to say it was a gift from the Princess Anastasia to my mother, or something of the kind, but I just don't know. Here it is, Nuri, keep it in this little wash-leather bag and if you need any money for Jason you must sell it; here is the address of an old-fashioned gem-merchant in London with whose firm my mother dealt."

She sat down on the edge of the divan, still peering into her handbag.

"So I am going?"

"Yes, my darling, you are going. The finding of this money has settled it. You must go at once, to-night, because don't imagine you are not going to have the police either come or send for you. You may think you and Landrake are above suspicion, but you aren't, you know. You're on the list, like everyone else Torgüt has known. And you two were the last to see him alive."

She gave him a sheet of paper upon which she had written some addresses, the boy's lodging in Oxford, his college, his bank, the friend who had stayed with them in the summer, a girl-friend whose address she had taken from a letter she had found in his room, and two English aunts of her mother of whom there was now only one left, who had once been to Istanbul to see them and with whom, in England, her mother had stayed in the country near Oxford shortly before she died. Then she brought out the key of the safe deposit in the City of London, labelled and with a list of the contents but Nuri bey refused to take it. He was surprised that she should trust him with it and reproved her for it. She said that she had known him long enough and that she trusted him entirely, but he begged her to keep the key. "If I need any more than you are giving me, I shall say so," he said firmly. "But I have no idea what I am going for to seek, what conditions I shall find, what problems, what expenses and I feel certain, Tamara, my lovely one, that you know more than you are telling me, which is nothing."

Her eyes avoided his but she returned practically: "Well, it is certain that I cannot go to England myself at present; that would indeed look suspicious."

Nuri bey seemed so bewildered that she laughed. "Come down out of the clouds or I shall regret sending you. I could have shot Torgüt as easily as anyone else." And so saying she produced a silk-wrapped object out of her capacious handbag and unfolded it, to reveal a small business-like-looking flat pistol. "With this," she added.

Nuri bey could say nothing.

"Being asleep is the easiest alibi in the world." She laid the pistol on the divan and took a cigarette from her own packet, lighting it with a small lighter. She was a pretty smoker, showing off her tiny hands and slim wrists. Leaning back against the wooden wall, she inhaled once or twice, looking at him through the smoke which she blew out in a thin, slow, deliberate stream. "You either are . . . or you aren't asleep. Who can prove it? I spend a lot of time in bed; Turkish women are not expected to be active, driving themselves about in their cars. In fact, the only place they are allowed to be active is in bed."

Nuri bey was shocked; he was, in fact, a prig because he had never had a chance to be anything else. It was rapidly being knocked out of him.

"So my alibi is: *I was in bed*, and, according to the Turks, that is exactly where I should be, it was meet and right so to be. And naturally, if I was in bed, I couldn't have been shooting my husband, tra la!" and Tamara burst into a delightful fit of laughter, more of a prolonged, deep chuckle, like water running over stones in a stream a long way down; she buried her head in a cushion and laughed it out whilst Nuri bey looked down at her: a changing man, he was like an "identikit" photograph of himself.

She sat up and dried her eyes with a tiny scrap of handkerchief which smelled entrancing. "Oh, dear," she said. "I'll be the death of you, won't I, as the old English cliché goes."

"Tamara," Nuri bey said deeply, after a long time. He wrestled with the words he wished to use which were in the nature of: If you could fall into my arms so easily, like a ripe plum, how am I to know whether you would do the same with any man in the abandoned manner you have shown with me? But all he could get out was another strangled "Tamara!"

It was as though she had read his thoughts exactly as he had thought them. "Yes, I see your point." She lighted another cigarette from the stub of the last one. "In a way it was reaction, the way I fell into your arms. But it was instinct, too, because you are the only man I know well, and trust absolutely. You are an old friend and a new lover."

He was pleased, he repeated her last remark twice, smiling now.

"Oh, Nuri! It's easy to see why you have never married. A woman isn't really a person, to you. But never mind, we'll change all that. Listen: I would not have stayed with Torgüt if we had not had a child. Jason was my reward for marrying Torgüt and I could never forget it and I stayed with him for that reason and none other. I have done my very best not to smother my good-looking son with love, because the poor creature is, in fact, the only thing I love now that my mother is dead. So I have never encouraged him to confide in me; we're just good friends, that's all. I'm his dear old Mum and if *I* were to go looking for him, the whole thing would be ridiculous. That's why I want you to go, darling. If you find him and set him on his feet again so that he can take his Finals in the middle of the summer, you can come back and *have me*, mistress, wife, slave, any way you want. If you don't . . . there won't be anyone for you to have because if something serious has happened to Jason, if, say, he doesn't live any more, then I shall be no good to you, an empty, useless old woman, with no joy left, and what good is a joyless woman to anyone?" Again the long thin stream of smoke.

Nuri bey's voice sounded inordinately deep when at last it came out: "So it is me . . . and Jason, or nothing?"

"Exactly, my darling."

She picked up the pistol, turning it over in her hand. "I ought to give you this gun but Landrake brought it back from London for what he and I thought were very good reasons. Those reasons still exist . . ."

"I will not take it. I should not know how to use it."

"Very well." She wrapped it up and put it away in her handbag. "If you think you need a gun you can always buy one in England."

When she left the stars were out, clean and polished in a deep blue sky. "Look," she pointed, "look where the Pleiades are, and Jupiter is still with you, my warrior, as a *Sagittarius*, that is lucky for you. There is Jupiter, see him? Shining as big and bright as ever he is seen. Don't keep your eyes on the stars, my darling, I will do that for you. But look at them sometimes and you will know that I, too, am watching Jupiter and thinking about you."

"I shall go to-night, immediately," Nuri bey said. "I shall go out to Yesilkoy by ordinary bus and wait at the airport for the next plane to Athens, or Rome, and go on from there to London."

"Good. That way you won't be here when they call to ask you more questions, as I am sure they will, probably tomorrow."

She paused, looking up into his face. "You won't be able to see the stars often in England but when you do, remember me."

"Remember you?" He bent his head and the farewell kiss he received sent him reeling back into his house.

Smiling, he started to fold his best suit: he had forgotten that he intended to have it cleaned.

PART TWO

That was Nuri bey

1

De Quincey, the decadent essayist, confesses that on the first time he took opium, in 1804: "It was Sunday afternoon, wet and cheerless; and a duller spectacle this earth of ours has not to show than a rainy day in London."

In one hundred and sixty years this state of affairs has not improved. Nuri bey came out of the B.E.A. bus terminus in South Kensington looking eagerly about him. Here he was, in the centre of the Western world, the fabulous city upon which the eyes of the world were constantly turned: London, whose streets were paved with gold, as they said.

He was walking down a dark canyon, the walls of which were caked with indescribable dirt, towering over him, frowning down. Along the middle of this gloomy gorge stood a stationary line of cars, buses and motor bicycles, all panting out petrol fumes which almost choked the new arrival. Rain was streaming down and he was enveloped in a grey plastic mackintosh he had just purchased at the airport.

"Paddington," he said to someone approaching under an umbrella.

"No spik Eenglish," was the reply.

"Paddington!" he shouted to a negro bus conductor who lolled on his platform looking at Nuri bey with a contemptuous grin. "Not this route, fella!"

"Paddington?" he asked three girls, all eating something out of a paper bag and straggling over the pavement.

"O . . . ou! You're going the wrong way," they said and went on their way, screaming with laughter.

A woman was approaching, briskly pushing a perambulator. Nuri bey had never seen one and he presumed it to be a machine in which babies are carried. "Paddington?" he asked hopefully. The woman was elderly and wore a severe uniform. "Sorry," and she brushed hastily past him.

Then he saw a policeman, he had heard all about London policemen; a kind of superhuman race, he believed. This one was standing in the middle of the road wearing a short black cloak from which the rain dripped copiously. Nuri bey stepped off the pavement and approached this Being: "Paddington?" The policeman stared at him coldly and for a long, long moment, whilst the drivers in the cars lined up, watched expressionless. "Don't you know," the policeman said, "that you never address a policeman on point duty?"

Nuri bey said, with a small bow: "I beg your pardon!"

The policeman looked at him even more closely. "Well, don't do it again," he said. He watched Nuri bey with a hard cold stare as he retreated to the wide pavement.

A few yards farther east the road widened into an open space in the centre of which stood a magnificent building which brought Nuri bey up with a sharp gasp of admiration. This was, surely, Buckingham Palace? Further investigation proved it to be the Natural History Museum and Nuri bey had to resist firmly its appeal in favour of the quest for Paddington. He had just decided that a *dolmus* was the answer when a taxi drove slowly past, the words TO HIRE illuminated on the roof and the driver was looking at him. He stepped forward, miraculously the driver stopped. "Paddington?" Inside, the door shut and London flashing past him, Nuri bey marvelled at the simplicity of it.

The aeroplane had been half-empty and, feeling lonely after the meal, Nuri bey had moved towards the rear of the plane and sat next to another Levantine-looking traveller who turned out to be Turkish. After a time Nuri bey had asked a number of questions about the arrival at the end of the journey and had finally asked how long the journey from London to Oxford would take. He was surprised to find that it was not on the outskirts of London, as he had believed, but some fifty miles into the country from a station with the name of Paddington. Though the fellow-traveller was by no means communicative, he had, at the end of their journey, vouchsafed that, if he was going to Oxford, the best hotel at which to stay would be the Randolph.

Nuri bey had spent much of his life seeing a kind of vision of Oxford in his mind; thus, as the train approached that fabulous city, he nervously asked the people in his carriage: "Oxford?" and on receiving curt nods, he looked eagerly out of the window at the darkening scene.

The train stopped as his gaze swept a field full of small stones somewhat resembling the Istanbul graveyards in that they were as derelict but flat. He also saw large round tank-like buildings which, undoubtedly, were some kind of pagan temples, for he knew Oxford to be a city of exceedingly ancient foundation.

"Please, what is that?" he asked a girl sitting next to him.

"The gas works," she answered politely.

Nuri bey pressed his face to the window. Where were the "dreaming spires"? After twenty minutes or so the train moved slowly into Oxford station and Nuri bey, quick to learn, leaped out, darted through the barrier, giving up his ticket, and into a taxi: "Randolph Hotel."

This was more like it: the grey brick, the terra-cotta decoration, the lancet windows, the gothic arches with the faintly Moorish flavour, the thick carpets, were greatly to his taste.

After a large dinner, a good night and a fabulous breakfast of which he ate almost everything on the menu, he dashed out for a quick look at the dreaming spires before getting down to work. These spires he never found: there were one or two towers from which came the sound of bells but of the dreaming spires he could only see one and that was the Martyrs Memorial, immediately outside his hotel, and not more than twenty-five feet high; it was certainly not dreaming, the traffic clashed and snarled around it and there were two public conveniences and a bicycle park within its precincts. He admired the turrets of Balliol College, squeezed his way between the cars down the Turl, peered into Lincoln and Jesus Colleges, turned into the High, turned again and walked between All Souls and the Radcliffe Camera across the quiet precinct. Here, on the old cobblestones, his heart was moved. In one or two places the stone had been cleaned and shone like guinea gold in the morning sun. As he walked towards the arch under the Old Bodleian he saw a doorway above which was written the information that it was the school of Moral Philosophy and this sent him into a short trance. He had passed the pompous expressionless face of William Pembroke, said to be a benefactor honourable and virtuous, clad from neck to knee in elaborate armour, and turning back to have a better look at the statue Nuri bey saw, quite definitely and certainly, The Man next to whom he had taken a seat for part of his air journey yesterday.

He averted his eyes instantly and, strolling towards the statue, appeared to be engrossed in what was inscribed on the stone plinth but without looking he could see the dark figure emerge from the arch, walk across the quadrangle and disappear through the opening at the opposite end.

Nuri bey circled William Pembroke and, not hurrying, sauntered through the passageways and out into Broad Street in front of the new Bodleian Library. On his left was Blackwell's bookshop, and to turn in that direction seemed the best possible move since he had spent a good part of his life wishing to enter that famous narrow little doorway. But before crossing the road he walked along the pavement until he was opposite the bookshop and from there he could see, some yards farther along, a large glass-covered map fixed to the wall for the benefit of visitors and studying it was the small dark overcoat-clad Man with toes turned, slightly absurdly, inwards. Nuri bey stopped, but not for long because he could see, quite clearly, that the sun shining on the street enabled The Man, standing back very slightly, to see cars and people as they passed reflected in the glass of the map and he had no doubt at all that The Man was watching him. He crossed the road boldly, opened the surprisingly small and insignificant door of the bookshop, and went inside.

There is no better place to hide than in this famous bookshop; though it looks tiny from outside, it is immense, with underground passages lined with books stretching away and away, eventually tunnelling under the old Library of Trinity College.

He panted to a standstill in the department of Theological books, from where he had a view right down the shop to the cash desk and there was an escape route up a small iron staircase behind him. He picked up a book at random and bent his head over it whilst still keeping a keen eye on the entrance. It was impossible that this could be a coincidence. If there were a coincidence, it was that Nuri bey had actually chosen to take the seat next to Him in the Comet. Now he remembered having caught a glimpse of Him at Yesilkoy as they had boarded the plane and again as they had strolled about the waiting lounge in Rome. He smiled his wry, lipless smile as he realised how The Man had saved Himself the trouble of following him along the streets of London, then to Paddington and Oxford, by recommending the Randolph hotel in that city. Fortunately, Nuri bey thought, oh, how fortunately, He had under-estimated him!

What was now more important was that Nuri bey should not underestimate The Man, because now He was standing in the entrance part of the shop, between Nuri bey and the cash desk, studying the table of new novels. Slowly, and apparently casually, He edged his way Nuri bey-wards.

Unfortunately Nuri bey was not one easily able to pass himself off as a common, or library, bookworm. He was as conspicuous as a daddy longlegs and, looking directly past The Man he was absolutely certain that He knew perfectly well that he was there and that He was going to hang around the entrance until he left, or murder him by strangulation, or any other quiet method, in a corner where sound would be deadened by the books. Boldly he put down the book which he had been apparently examining and walked purposefully back through the shop towards the entrance. Here he found a staircase and ran lightly up it, one flight, two flights, to the second floor. He went up as far as he could and penetrated into a department where, surely, no one ever went. There was a tiny window which Nuri bey opened and then looked out over the garden below. There seemed to be no possible exit from the back of the shop. There was nothing for it but to tire out his follower. He took out a book and propped himself against the shelves pretending to read. He heard the bells striking midday. After a half-hour more had passed he began to feel hungry and, longing to know if The Man was still waiting down below, he started to stroll back to Mankind. He took a long time to get himself down two flights of stairs and was about boldly to descend to the ground floor and bolt out into the street when he saw The Man mounting the stairs towards him, fortunately with bent head. He dived into a small opening, not more than a yard in width, between bookshelves and leading to a very small, airless space devoted to secondhand travel and cookery books. He hesitated for a moment and then slid through another incredibly narrow opening and found himself outside a door with frosted glass panels. He darted inside; it was a neat, staff lavatory with handbasin, coloured soap, clean folded handtowel, and tiny window. He locked the door and leaned against it. All sound was muffled but he heard, through the window, two clocks chiming one. He was hungry; it was evident that he would have to come out of his hiding place sooner or later.

At this time he did not think that The Man had seen him but he waited another half-hour before carefully opening the door and looking out. On the right was an office, a dead end. He decided to emerge into the main shop and escape. Closing the door noiselessly behind him he crept back through the opening between the bookshelves and, as he did so, he thought that if his pursuer had been fat he would never have been able to slide through the small space. Unaccountably the electric light had gone out but there was enough daylight from a window by the opening to see fairly well. His pursuer was standing in the small stuffy cave, not reading but apparently alert, listening, waiting for him to glide silently out between the old books. Both pursuer and pursued started violently.

"Good morning," Nuri bey managed to croak in his own language. "Why do you follow me?" he said and, involuntarily, without any intention of doing so, his hand moved towards his pocket. Instantly The Man whipped out a small revolver.

So soon, Nuri bey thought sadly, so soon! He put up his hands but simultaneously let out with his foot, sending the absurd little creature crashing and sprawling backwards against the books. He unarmed him as gently as a mother removing a dummy from her babe's mouth.

"Now," he said, "please tell me why you are following me, or I shall fire."

"That would be unwise," The Man replied, "because half the shop would hear the sound and come running."

"I do not care," Nuri bey returned, and in the mood which was a direct descent from the young Circassian warrior, breast-fed till he was ten, without taking his eyes from The Man, he unhitched the safety catch of the automatic in his hand and fired it deliberately about two feet wide, into the poor, harmless books. It was like firing inside a thickly padded box; the revolver gave Nuri bey a great dig in the ribs and the sound waves for a moment knocked him silly. The air in the restricted space rocked and vibrated and there was so much dust that Nuri bey knew he must sneeze.

"Take off your shoes," he said steadily. He got rid of his sneeze whilst The Man undid His shoes. "And now your trousers," he ordered. The Man did as He was told and threw them at Nuri bey's feet. "Now pick them up and give them to me," he demanded. After a moment's hesitation The Man did so.

"You may go," Nuri bey said graciously. He backed away through the opening behind and back into the lavatory where he opened the window wider and threw the trousers and shoes out. Not bothering to look where they fell, he emerged to find The Man, bereft and bewildered, where he had left him.

"Once more," Nuri bey said, "tell me who you are and why you are following me."

The Man shook his head. "Yok!" Which is a very definite Turkish no.

"I shall shoot you if you don't."

The Man shook his head, again opening his hands in a gesture of resignation. Nuri bey repeated what he had said in Turkish. The Man replied also in Turkish. "Worse than shooting may happen to me if I speak, so shoot if you must."

Nuri bey gave him a long, searching look, then he put the revolver into his own pocket.

"Farewell, then," he said and slipped out between the books into the open shop, wearing the smooth expression of one who has decided not to buy a book to-day. There was no one about and complete silence. Nuri bey went down the last flight of stairs into the entrance part of the shop; there was nobody sitting at the cash desk, the shop was empty. He went to the door, which was latched, he turned the knob and unlocked the door, he slipped out into the street and as he shut the door after him he saw the small handwritten notice: CLOSED BETWEEN 1 AND 2.15 P.M.

2

In fifteen minutes he had checked out of the Randolph, telling the receptionist that he had much enjoyed his stay but was obliged to return to London unexpectedly.

Several hundred yards along St. Giles he was arrested by a nostalgic smell of fried onions and on a corner noticed a small restaurant which he entered, and ate what everybody else was eating with their fingers, a fried hamburger steak and onions in a split white muffin. With his second cup of coffee and his third muffin, he had not solved the question of why The Man had pointed his revolver; was it a threat or had he seriously meant to murder him then and there? If the latter, Nuri bey's admiration for him was great. The Man had the advantage of Nuri bey in knowing that the bookshop closed between one and two-fifteen, and furthermore, he must have known from the rather one-sided conversation in the Comet that Nuri bey had never been to England before, and would be unlikely to know anything about lunch-hour closing. It was the perfect time and the perfect place to kill Nuri bey.

But why?

He thought hard but he could not remember having displayed his note-stuffed pocket book and thought it exceedingly unlikely that he would have done so. He did not look a person of means and if The Man had intended to kill him for money, it was taking a big risk for small gain.

What then?

It could only be that it was someone who knew him by sight, who had seen him about in Istanbul, or had had him pointed out by someone in that city; someone who had come deliberately with him on the plane to watch his movements; someone who, when mounting the stairs in the bookshop to look for him had seen him and had followed him into the book-cave and waited for him to reappear, *knowing* that there was no other exit; someone, in fact, who knew the city of Oxford well, who knew that Nuri bey would go into Blackwell's bookshop as certainly as he knew that he would also go into the Bodleian Library; someone, in fact, who knew the habits of Nuri bey.

He put his elbows on the pink plastic table-top and held his head. The Man had not intended to murder him, because he could quite easily have done so in Istanbul, much more easily, in fact. He had been following Nuri bey because He wanted information and when He had cornered him in Blackwell's He had been about to extract the information from him.

So, on the whole, Nuri bey realised, he had not been so clever. It had been a mistake to act on impulse and disarm the poor little weasel without finding out what he wanted. Not so clever.

Deeply depressed by his bad beginning, Nuri bey picked up his carpet bag and left the coffee bar to find that there was a small hotel next door. He went in, discovered there was a room available, engaged it, left his carpet bag and strode out into St. Giles purposefully. The roles were changed, armed now with a passable gun containing five bullets, Nuri bey was going to follow The Man, abandoning, for the moment, his intention of calling on the Dean.

It was now shortly after two-fifteen and The Man would have been found by the returning bookshop staff and no doubt his trousers and shoes would have been retrieved. It would have been more clever, Nuri bey thought, if he had stuffed them behind a row of books, but unfortunately the bookshelves had ended beyond the opening to the lavatory.

He ascertained from a passer-by that the large building at the end of St. Giles was the Taylorian and that the Ashmolean Museum was round the corner immediately across the road from the Randolph. The steps of the Museum were a splendid place from which to observe people going in and out of the hotel and he had not been standing at this vantage point more than a quarter of an hour when The Man bustled round the corner and into the hotel, wearing his trousers and shoes. Then passed three hours and three-quarters during which Nuri bey suffered agonies of impatience watching the entrance, strolling backwards and forwards across the corner of the courtyard in front of the Museum so that he could move about without taking his eyes from the doorway. Though wearing his grey plastic mackintosh, he was extremely cold and uncomfortable when The Man, bustling again, came down the hotel steps and walked away round the corner. Nuri bey was after him like a hare and with as little subtlety; there was no dodging into doorways, he marched along the crowded streets not more than ten yards behind, finally up the steps of a building which, upon entering he knew at once to be a police station. The Man did not look behind him and Nuri bey followed him. There were several people leaning on the counter, talking across it to uniformed but hatless policemen on the other side. One of these curiously undressed-looking policemen came forward, saying to The Man: "Can I help you, sir?"

"I am seeking a young man who is a student here."

"And the name?"

"Jason Yenish, a student at Latimer College."

"And your name, sir?"

"Arnika." He brought out His passport. "I am a native of Turkey . . ." He was now more relaxed and leaned on the counter on one arm, thus expanding His field of vision; from the side of His eye He saw someone standing immediately behind Him and whipped round with a cry of alarm. "This man, this man . . ." He was beside himself with anger as He pointed a shaking finger at Nuri bey. "Officer, he tried this morning to kill me."

Nuri bey was at his most smooth; half-smiling, he looked pityingly at his accuser. "Not at all, not at all," he said calmly.

The one who is calm always has the advantage over the one who is angry. There were two policemen now and they were paying more attention to Nuri bey than to Arnika bey though at the same time keeping a sharp eye on the latter. Accusations foamed from the thick lips of Arnika bey whilst Nuri bey calmly, still faintly smiling, added fuel to the flame by slowly shaking his head from side to side, maddeningly. They were taken into an ante-room, where things were gradually, if not sorted out, at least given a semblance of order. Nuri bey stated that he, too, had been asked to come to Oxford to look for the boy Yenish, by his mother; his father had died suddenly and the boy's presence was required in Istanbul. Arnika was unable to explain why he wanted to find the boy; the police told them both that the disappearance had been reported by the college authorities, it was not the first time an undergraduate had "disappeared." No one was unduly alarmed, no foul play was suspected; the young man had simply failed to turn up at the beginning of the Michaelmas term. The police had his description and were on the look-out for him.

Arnika again started raving about Nuri bey, saying that he had stolen a valuable revolver; as this was not quite compatible with the accusation of murder, they treated the information calmly. Nuri bey, hoping that the bulge in his pocket was not too apparent but thankful to the marrow that he had kept on his grey plastic mackintosh since he had left the Randolph, brought out the small notebook in which he had copied the addresses Tamara had given him and said that he was on the point of calling on two elderly relatives of the missing boy: "Lady Mercia and Lady Miranda Mossop of Coverley Place, near Oxford."

The respect of the two police officers was now quite plain. Early in the New Year, Lady Miranda had died, poor old lady, they said. But Lady Mercia was still wonderful, and their faces glowed with the pleasure and respect the English feel towards the very ancient. Nuri bey had played his ace of trumps and won, game and rubber. He showed his passport, gave the address of his hotel as the Randolph, and wrote down the names of the two police officers who had been so helpful. He buttoned up his mackintosh; ignoring Arnika, he bowed to the two policemen and left, with the shining accusations of Arnika still sounding in his ears.

But there were more important things to do than to go at once to see an old lady.

3

My beloved,
This is the first time in my life I have written a love letter. You have got into my blood-stream, you beautiful-as-the-moon-woman and you pass through my head, my heart and my lungs three times every minute. For the love of Allah take care of yourself. I realise that there is desperation amongst those whom we must call our enemies, they want something and they mean to get it. I have been here forty-eight hours and have had good fortune though nothing as yet that I can say to cause you to rejoice. Please write c/o Poste Restante, Oxford. Tamara, my lovely white one, I love you.

Your Nuri

Salud Landrake! Mon brave,
This, I see, is, as you say, a question of Life and Death. I have been followed from Istanbul by *Arnika*, armed. Who and why is he? All I understand is that he and I are looking for the same Person. I am at present at a hotel, 200*a* St. Giles, Oxford, but may leave at any moment if necessary. Please write at once to Poste Restante, Oxford.

To-day I have been to see the Dean of the College and I cannot say it was a fruitful visit. He did not show any horror or shock at my news that the boy has not been heard of. He stated it to be "one of those things"; what did he mean, my friend? I asked to see the headmaster (Warden he is called) but was told he was unable to see me. I asked the Dean if I could see the boy's personal tutor and was given the address. The Dean seemed glad to see me go.

The tutor I found to be slightly mad but of good intent. He said that the boy was brilliant and therefore liable to do anything.

He called him a natural, three or four times, and there was much that I could not comprehend. He called him a sentimentalist, an idealist and other names of a high order. He is reading modern languages: Russian, and the tutor said he would get a Number One degree as a "walk-over" if he had not "gone off the rails." He said the boy had a brilliant future if he could only keep his eyes off the stars. You can imagine that I did not mention that his mother never looked at anything else! He told me that the boy had many friends who had all been questioned as to his whereabouts but they had all been "loyal to a man." No one was saying anything. He said I would get nothing out of any of them. He talked so fast and said so much that I missed most of it and (even now I can scarcely believe it) he had an infant beside the window in an infant-carriage; this small thing screamed most of the time I was there; he kept picking it up and throwing it up in the air and catching it while he talked. Finally he gave it a small Russian pocket dictionary; I came away quickly after that but even before I left, the toothless thing had eaten a good half. This tutor had dirty clothes and wild eyes which rolled strangely in his head as he talked. Two young men came in while I was there and I felt obliged to go though there was much which I left unexplained.

Make haste, my friend, to send all you know about *Arnika* and rest assured that your friend Nuri has been threatened but is now, himself, armed with an automatic gun of Belgium make and has already fired it, once. Not to kill *Arnika* but to frighten him, an easy matter. I have found a gun shop where they sold me a dozen bullets to fit the gun; they did so without surprise or comment, as though I were buying buttons to sew on my shirt.

Nuri

Farther along the road, Nuri bey found the entrance to the ladies' college; he went in on tiptoe with a great deal more awe than he would enter St. Sophia. A long stone-flagged passage stretched ahead, a few girls walked up or down but they were of such terrifying aspect that Nuri bey did not dare to ask anything of them. Some wore black stockings and had skirts many inches above their knees so that Nuri bey felt they must have lost their skirts. Some wore their hair piled as high as XVIII Century wigs, others had their hair hanging on their shoulders and some wore it over their faces in a kind of yashmak but more concealing and these Nuri bey took to be the more ladylike and shy ones. All looked at him but their eyes strayed away with no more interest than if they had alighted upon a hat rack. The ones who were not walking singly were talking in groups and no one seemed to be listening to anyone else. A small bun-shaped woman hurried down the passage, looking at him with inquiry in her expression.

"Can I help you?" she asked.

"Miss Hannah Benson," Nuri bey mouthed and his eyes opened very widely when he was told to go to her room, number 16 at the end of the passage upstairs. There was much noise coming from within Room Number 16 and someone shouted "Come in," to his knock. A den of lions would have been easier to deal with; weak at the knees, he walked in.

Three girls were crouched round an electric radiator, a record player was beating out a metallic thumping sound and a fourth girl was standing by herself shaking from head to foot, her head, her mouth, her eyes, her shoulders, her breasts, her stomach, her . . . Nuri bey took root, losing all consciousness of time and place.

"Turn off that thing!" someone shouted. "Hallo there! Who are you?"

The girl turned off the player and gave Nuri bey a wide smile. "That was The Shake," she said unnecessarily.

"Who do you want to see?"

Nuri bey pulled himself together. He bowed. "I am Nuri Iskirlak from Istanbul; I wish to see Miss Hannah Benson."

She emerged from the throng looking so like the only young woman of her kind that Nuri bey had ever known that he greeted her with enthusiasm but there was no answering eagerness on her part. She sat fiddling nervously with her hair while Nuri bey told her why he had come: Jason Yenish's father had died suddenly and as a friend of the family he had been asked to come to Oxford to bring him home.

"Why come to me?"

"Your name and address was given to me by his mother. She thought you were, that is, might be, a friend."

"No, not at all," the girl snapped. "I haven't seen him since the summer term. He's gone down."

"Gone down?"

"Left Oxford."

"But he is in his final year," Nuri bey exclaimed, "his Final Examinations in four months' time."

"That's up to him," she shrugged.

She was a pretty girl and Nuri bey, still standing because he had not been asked to sit, looked at her sadly: so young and so untender! One of the other girls scrambled to her feet and asked him to sit; the two others made a few pleasant remarks and suggested he would like some tea but Nuri bey, taking his cue from the hardened profile of Hannah, now turned from him and silent, said he had better go. He apologised for disturbing them, bowed again formally and left regretfully.

Thinking furiously he took great strides along the passage, down the stairs, along the ground floor passage and let himself out through the big double doors. As he walked past the dining hall towards the gate someone caught him up: "Mr. Iskirlak." It was the Shaking-one and she was carrying about eleven books under her arm. She dropped several in her excitement and Nuri bey stooped to pick them up.

"Hannah doesn't know I've followed you but I felt I must, you looked so unhappy. You see . . . she absolutely adored Jason and he was pretty keen on her. They've been together ever since they both came up. Jason asked her to stay with him at his home in Istanbul last summer but she couldn't because she had to go to America to see her father; her parents are separated so it was a matter of *having* to go. Since she wrote to say she couldn't go, she hasn't heard a word from him. Of course, she thinks he's found someone else, one of those lush Turkish girls you hear about." She was quite breathless with talking.

"Could you spare the time for a cup of coffee?" Nuri bey asked formally. She couldn't but she would, so he took her to the coffee bar beside his hotel and they talked for half an hour. It was a pleasant time, the girl was charming and friendly, and Nuri bey listened with attention to the girlish gossip, she was a great talker. Jason was popular, he had many friends and led a social life; he was a member of several societies. "In a way," she said, "he's a bit of a do-gooder."

"In what way do you mean?"

"Good-natured. He'd say he would be secretary of a society because no one else wanted to be, and then things would get a bit much for him, you know, entertaining speakers, tearing round, whipping up subscriptions and that kind of thing, and then, last summer term, he got mixed up with an awful beat set."

"What is that?"

"Well, you'd have to know a lot more about Oxford to understand; all Left Wing: some of them are anarchists, and some of them poets, and some of them writers of articles in pamphlets that no one can understand; very *avant garde*."

Nuri bey was a fascinated audience, it would be difficult not to tell him everything one could think up. She went on glibly: "They aren't bad but they behave sort of *anti*."

"Anti?"

"Anti everything. They go against the stream; they dress oddly, for one thing; some of them are vegetarians *on principle*, oh, they've got very high principles, some of them may be the future 'village Hampdens' but a lot of them are absolutely phoney, layabouts; they smoke marihuana and do everything just for the kicks."

"But what do the college authorities do about it?"

She shrugged. "It takes all sorts, you know."

"But Jason wasn't . . . like that!"

"Oh, no!" She paused. "I'm telling you everything, aren't I? You wouldn't catch me talking to my parents like this." She hugged herself delightedly: "It's your Eastern charm, Mr. Nuri. Perhaps I shouldn't tell you this but . . ." Tantalisingly she stopped.

"If I am to find this young man I ought to know everything."

"I'm gossiping. I don't think what I'm saying has the slightest thing to do with where he is."

"Continue, please."

"Well, I'll tell you first that I think Hannah was Jason's girl; I can't say Jason was the faithful sort, being Eastern, but on the other hand I'm not saying he was a womaniser."

"A what?"

"Laying every girl he came across, but there's this awful girl *everyone* knows. She's nineteen and she's had two children, Lord knows who the fathers are. She doesn't seem to have any parents or relatives or any proper home and she's here . . . well . . . as a kind of Freshman's Folly."

"What do you mean?"

"First year undergraduates. Some of them are straight from school, with their tuck still round their mouths; they're goggle-eyed when they see a girl like her."

"Beautiful?"

"No. Dirty; dressed, well, you wouldn't believe it, long hairy jumpers down to her knees and about an inch of skirt showing, but somehow or other terribly, terribly sexy."

Nuri bey had been so shocked that now he was about to come up on the other side; shocked beyond shock, he was learning a kind of cold, analytical calm.

"Go on."

"Well, these Freshmen, I mean the odd one or two, of course, they can't wait to jump into bed with her; well, that is just an expression, you can call it a roll in the hay or a scramble in the shrubbery . . ."

"You mean, sexual intercourse," Nuri bey said sternly.

"Um. Then, all of a sudden, they're men of the world, and you see them swaggering down the Broad. But it's sad, isn't it, because there are such a lot of us nice girls who want a nice boy friend." There was a long, slightly nostalgic pause while she toyed with the spoon in her saucer. "I'm in my third year," she said, "and I feel as old as hell; I feel I've seen it all and know it all. But I've had a marvellous time up at University, I wouldn't have missed it for worlds."

"Why did we start to talk about this girl?"

"Oh, yes. Well, Jason sort of took her up."

"No! I hope not."

"Well, I, personally, don't think he wanted her like the others. I think he had a sort of fascinated interest in her as a human being. She is pretty different from anything you have in Turkey, I expect?" She looked at him shyly.

"Very different."

"I think that he was a kind of proselyte, trying to reform her. Of course," she added cynically, "these proselyte-types often want to cut off the joint for themselves, I don't trust them."

"What is the name of this female?"

"Ronda. She's been up before the City magistrates once or twice, for obstructing and for larking about on Guy Fawkes Night. There is a rumour that she's been up for something else and that she's on probation, and it may be true because, when I come to think about it, she hasn't been seen around recently."

Kindly, and at length she explained the probation system. "But of course," she said thoughtfully, "it could be she is out of circulation at the moment because she may be in the family way again. You would have thought, wouldn't you, that she had learned by now how not to?"

Probation officer!

When he had wrung The Shaker or rather, when he had helped The Shaker to wring herself quite dry, he hired a car, dropped her at her tutor's, drove round to the police station, to the magistrate's court, to a hospital, to a small house behind the station, to an approved school on the outskirts of the city and back to the magistrate's court at the speed of sound. At last he found the probation officer he required coming down the steps of the Court, her arm in that of a woman who looked in the last stages of human misery.

"Miss Smith?" he asked eagerly.

"I'll be with you in half a tick, I'll just run this soul home." He would have liked to ask her to take tea with him at the Randolph but decided not to risk meeting Arnika again and chose a tea shop in High Street.

"Our work is strictly confidential, you know," she reminded Nuri bey, "but, of course, if there is any way in which I can help you to find the young man you are seeking, I will certainly do so."

"The only reason I have come to you," he said, "is that I believe he was interested in a girl, rather notorious in this city, who is one of those in your care." She began to look wary, she put down the half scone and butter she had been about to eat and looked straight-faced across the tiny table.

"What girl?"

"Does 'Ronda' convey anything to you?"

"Quite a lot. Apart, of course, from being an enchanting little mountain town in Spain . . ."

"Could you, might I, would it be possible . . ." Nuri bey floundered. If he had been the probation officer he would strongly have resented his questioning.

She started to eat her scone and butter. "I could tell you quite a lot about Ronda, Mr. Iskirlak, but perhaps, first, there is something you could tell me about her."

"Only to-day have I heard of her existence," he assured her, "and I am interested only in that she was an acquaintance of the young man I seek."

Miss Smith finished her scone. "She is one of the wild ones," she murmured. "Her mother turned her out of the house when she was fifteen. She is the mother of two children; with her first the country did all they could to help her but that poor baby . . ." she broke off. "Never mind, we got him satisfactorily adopted in the end. The second time Mother Government isn't so keen to help unmarried mothers, but somehow, someone got her to consent to have the child adopted before she saw it. She was soon back on the old track. I . . ." she smiled, even laughed a little, "I'm quite fond of her because, and I'm not trying to be funny, she's so consistently bad; bad absolutely through and through."

"But is not your Christian teaching that no one is quite bad?"

"Indeed yes, Mr. Iskirlak. But Ronda is bad because she can't help being bad, and she knows it, and I know it, and everybody else knows it; that, possibly, is her attraction for all these young men. But Ronda is a particularly sad case."

"Hopeless?"

She laughed a little again. "We never admit that anyone is hopeless, never; there are some things Ronda isn't. For instance, she's greedy but she's not mean. She's unkind but she's not cruel. She's absolutely abandoned and does exactly what she wants to do when she wants it and she's not sorry afterwards but she does admit that she wishes she were not like that; she does agree that there's no future in it but she can't help herself. She hates authority and despises anyone over twenty-three but she does realise that we are trying to help her and wishes that we were more successful." She chuckled again. "It's a fascinating job, this, if you don't let it get you down. I can tell you, Ronda is the most intractable case, I mean *young* case, I have had, so far. I won't let myself think she's hopeless because, if I do, she'll feel it, somehow, and then it really will be hopeless but . . ." She looked serious and suddenly very sad. "I try not to let things affect me personally but I think Ronda has given me the worst knock of my career, so far. She's been smoking Indian Hemp since she was fifteen, now she's gone on to something worse, oh, much much worse!"

Nuri bey was so excited he almost knocked over the table, laden with tea things, but he managed to keep it under control.

"This young man you are looking for would be very unlikely to have anything much to do with a girl like Ronda, though I don't say the clever ones aren't sometimes the naughtiest! Now I really must be on my way; thank you for the delightful tea and I do wish I could have been more help. Just let me jot down your young man's name." She scribbled in her notebook as Nuri bey paid the bill.

"And could you give me an address to find her?"

She rose and went towards the door; Nuri bey hastened to open it for her. Out in the High she said: "I've left my car just round there, so good-bye . . ."

"Her address?"

She looked infinitely pained. She sighed heavily: "Oh, Mr. Iskirlak . . ."

Nuri bey caught her gloved hand. "Please, please, Miss Smith."

"You're very persuasive, aren't you?"

A bus laden with rush-hour crowds lurched past and the rest of what she said was hidden. She hesitated a long moment, looking down at her gloved hands. "I'm deeply ashamed at my inefficiency and I'm terribly worried about her: the truth is . . . *I can't find Ronda.* I shall probably get the sack, which I couldn't bear, but she's slipped through my fingers. There is a warrant out for her arrest for breach of probation order and *I haven't seen her since October*, so there!"

She hurried away.

4

Nuri bey spent a desperate night; time and again he woke shaking with some nameless fear and sense of shock. He got out of bed many times to look at the stars but the sky was overcast. The bells seemed to him more insistent than the cry of the muezzin in his own country. At dawn the sky cleared and he saw the morning star, as bright as a miniature sun; he put on his clothes and went out, taking a tremendous walk and orientating himself to the point of having a map of the city in his head; he saw early morning fauna such as very old gentlemen on tricycles, monks, and young men scantily dressed, running with great breath balloons emerging from their mouths into the frosty air.

At breakfast he decided that his first move of the day would be to visit Anthony Harp, the friend who spent a holiday with Jason Yenish in the summer. The address given him by Tamara took him to a small house in a quiet row. He rang the bell and waited. He rang again. After a further wait, a tousled young man dressed in pyjamas and a dressing gown which he had clearly just thrown on, opened the door. Harp had gone to breakfast in college, he said.

At the college entrance the porter told him that breakfast was still in progress; Nuri bey studied the notice board. "Who exactly were you wanting?" the porter asked. "Mr. Anthony Harp; yes, he's having breakfast in hall. He'll be out soon."

"May I look round?"

"Certainly, sir."

Nuri bey wandered across the quad and through an archway into a large garden. The turf was a miracle of delicacy; the soil had been hoed for so many years that it was fine as sifted flour and no weed found it tenable; nothing much was showing above ground but Nuri bey felt awed by the quietude, the peace and the odd feeling he received of the garden being haunted. There was a kind of unearthly stillness with no breath of wind stirring. He felt a coldness creeping over him, a beginning of what Landrake called "one of Nuri's turns."

In the centre of the vast lawn was a curious breast-shaped hill, covered with shrubs. He could see railings too amongst the shrubs. He moved across the grass towards it; was it some kind of huge grave, or memorial, or Anglo-Saxon remain? He pushed up through the undergrowth and at the top found a gravestone, green-stained, cracked, broken in places. It had once been surrounded by railings, some of which still stood, the rest lying rusted and crumbling here and there on the bare, hard, black earth. The carved inscription was obscured by a greenish growth and, bending forward he tried to read it, but the light was poor, obscured as it was by the undergrowth. He now felt so cold that he knew it was unnatural but the sound of twigs crackling as someone drew near brought him back to earth suddenly; he moved a hand to his pocket and turned the safety catch of the gun to the off position; grasping the gun still in his pocket, he flashed round expecting to see the square uncompromising shape of Arnika. But he gave an involuntary shout of shock at the sight of a tall, black-clad figure wearing a strange flat hat with a hanging tassel, a white clerical collar and a greyish-white face showing a look of alarm equal to that of Nuri bey's.

"Oh, I beg your pardon, I do beg your pardon," the apparition stammered.

Nuri bey, on his side, had pardon to beg, and did so, bowing.

"I'm s . . . so s . . . sorry . . . I thought, that is, I thought perhaps," but the cleric was not able quite to get out what it was he thought. His embarrassment was so great that Nuri bey allowed him his apologies as he backed away through the undergrowth, bowing nervously and hurrying away across the lawn like an injured blackbird with wing-tops drooping.

Nuri bey's enthusiasm for exploring ran out. Warm now, he went back to the porter's office.

"Met the Dean, did you?" the porter chuckled. "He's Invigilating at Prelims this morning. That's why he's dressed up like that," he explained to the bewildered foreigner. "He's always snooping around, you never know where he'll turn up. Discipline's his job."

The porter said that Mr. Harp would be sure to be along in a minute or so and exchanged pleasantries, in the course of which Nuri bey told him that he had come from Turkey. The porter said that it was funny, two Turkish gentlemen turning up in two days and the only one he'd ever had the pleasure of meeting was an undergraduate, half Turk, he was. And Nuri bey said, oh, indeed! And the porter said, yes, Mr. Yenish had gone down now but he'd been up a couple of years. Nuri bey did not have to ask who the other Turkish gentleman had been: he knew.

"There's Mr. Harp, just coming," the porter said.

A group of young men was approaching and the one that was Anthony Harp, at the nod from the porter, detached himself and came over to Nuri bey. "Do you want *me*?"

"Excuse me, are you not a friend of Jason Yenish? Then could you kindly spare me a few minutes of your time?" Having moved away from the porter's straining ears, Harp said there was very little he could tell him that would be of any help. Nuri bey said that anything at all that he could say about his friend Jason would be of help. He had been sent by Jason's mother; Jason's father had died suddenly and it was important to find the young man.

Harp was shocked, it was easy to see. He was a pleasant-looking young man and now he looked worried and suggested that they go to the Kemp and talk it over. At first he was wary but Nuri bey seemed so grave and anxious that he relaxed and began to talk frankly about his friend. He had a lot to say about how much he enjoyed his holiday in Istanbul, how kind the Yenishes had been and, finally, how worried he was about Jason. Indeed, all his friends were worried and spent much of their time talking about him.

"Then you have no idea what has happened to him?"

"We've all got our ideas, but some of them are pretty wild."

"When did you last see him?"

"I've seen him once since the vac., the day we came up at the beginning of the Michaelmas term. He was walking along the pavement and I passed in my car. I waved and he waved back; I knew I'd be meeting him in hall, if not sooner. That's the last I saw of him. Later on I went round to his lodging and the Oxmarm said he seemed to have gone, but left all his things. Naturally I thought he didn't like his rooms and that he went off to the Delegacy to find an address of other lodgings, but no."

"Why has there not been a big outcry?"

"I suppose because undergraduates can behave in an odd way. It's not unknown for them to disappear."

"Reely!" When Nuri bey was surprised he sounded very foreign.

"They work too hard; their minds go, if you ask me. Not that I think for a moment that happened to Jason. But there have been some enquiries about him; the police know he's missing. The college authorities think he's just hopped it and the Oxmarm can't think about anything but the money she's not getting for the room. Jason was unlucky in his lodging, his Oxmarm is a real terror. What has Jason's father died of?"

"He's been murdered," Nuri bey said with a certain grim pleasure. "Shot dead." He sat back and enjoyed the effect of his news.

"No wonder you want to find Jason," Harp said at last. "Glory, what a thing! Do you think it has anything to do with his disappearance?"

"Do you?"

"How could I possibly even try a guess? I got the impression that though Jason was perfectly civil to his father, he disapproved of him, somehow."

"In what way?"

"I can't explain it any better. He never talked to me about him. His mother is a perfect poppet, of course," and from his smile Nuri bey gathered that he was paying her a compliment.

He went on to say that at the end of his holiday he chose to return to England by boat so that he could see something of the Ægean; he flew home from Venice. Jason had flown back to England from Istanbul on the first day of term. There was a long pause. Harp eyed Nuri bey. "No, no!" he said, "definitely not that. It's not the way Jason would deal with a situation, however frightful or shocking."

"Did he get into a bad set here?"

He smiled wryly: "If you'd call the set I'm in a bad set? I dunno."

"Wild young men, anarchists . . . vegetarians—"

"Hey! You've been talking around. Yes, well, Jason was interested in everything. He did frat, I mean make friends a bit with the people you're thinking of but he wasn't one of them, not at all."

"Tell me more."

"Jason is one of those lucky people who can, who could, I should say, get a First without doing more than a normal amount of work. His home life was bilingual and he wrapped his tongue round Russian from the moment he could talk, and they had an old Russian woman who had been his mother's nurse and acted as Jason's nurse when he was a kid, the *Babushka*, they called her. They talked Turkish in the family, but his mother always spoke English to him when they were alone. In addition to all that, he's extremely bright. So 'Modern Languages' don't present any big problem."

"You mean, clever?"

"Um. The rest of us, in our set, if we mean to get a degree at all, have to work like . . . like, well, the amount of work we've got to do in our last year is fantastic, and if you've got only an average brain, there's no time for larking about, like they used to do in the old days when my father was up. It's one long, bloody grind. I think Jason got a bit bored with all the work his friends were doing, he amused himself with the people you've been calling a 'bad set.'"

"Now, what else can you tell me about him?"

"I could go on all day; Jason is my best friend."

"What can you tell me that could help me to find him?"

"He's got some relations, two great-great aunts, about a hundred years old. No, one's died recently, it was in the papers around New Year but there's one left. I went to see her when Jason didn't appear. She doesn't know anything but it might be worth calling on her, not that she can supply you with any more background information than I can."

"And there's his girl-friend."

Harp nodded. "Um, Hannah, she's okay."

"I've been here since Sunday," Nuri bey said, "and so far I can't say I'm exactly getting on. What would you say if you knew that someone followed me from Istanbul and who, when he knew that I knew he was following me, pointed a revolver in my face?"

"In Oxford?"

"In Oxford."

"I'd say look out. If they've killed Mr. Yenish, they'd kill you probably."

Nuri bey patted his pocket. "Fortunately I have the gun here, though I understand there is no difficulty about the buying of another. I've never seen this man Arnika before but I chanced to sit down next him in the plane, when I got a bit restless. I had a conversation with him as to how to get to Oxford, so I realised that it had been a coincidence indeed when I found him following me around the town. After all that, I followed him," he smiled grimly, "to Oxford police station and stood behind him only to hear . . ." He leaned forward conspiratorially and Harp laughed: "My word, you sound like James Bond!"

"Who is he?"

"A national hero. Well?"

". . . only to hear him ask for Jason Yenish, a student at Latimer College. Had I been more careful, as your national hero would have been, and not pressed forward so that he turned and saw me, I might have learned a good deal more; as it was, we both went into an anteroom with two policemen and it came out we *both* sought Jason Yenish, a situation which must have seemed ridiculous to your policemen."

"Oh, no, not necessarily. A chap is missing, two people come from his country to find him."

"But not both at the same time, each apparently ignorant of the other's move. I think Arnika followed me because he knew, or thought he knew, that I was coming to find Jason. I think they have tried to find Jason before now, possibly to kill him as they killed his father. So now I am doubly in difficulty because, if I find Jason, it may be that I shall expose him to the same fate as his father and, if that is so . . ." Nuri bey gave one of his extensive shrugs, "everything has gone; the warm, strong light which shines on certain people . . . it will be extinguished. So, my friend Anthony Harp, (you are my friend, are you not?) you will be very, very careful, will you not?"

5

Nuri bey waited so long on the doorstep after he had rung the bell that he turned away, thinking that no one was at home. As he moved down the path the door opened and someone called after him: "Anything you want?"

Yes, there was something he wanted. He wished to speak to someone about Mr. Yenish. The door opened more widely.

"Are you the Oxmarm?" Nuri bey asked politely.

"The what?"

"The . . ." Nuri bey was about to repeat the word but she said: "You're a foreign gentleman, I see. Have you come from Turkey, then?"

Nuri bey admitted that, in fact, he had and she invited him into the sitting-room to the left of the front door, upon the sofa of which she had clearly been lying because an eiderdown was thrown aside. She was wearing slippers with a rim of pink fur round the ankles and in her corn-coloured hair there were strange pieces of metal. She said that she had been far from well and should really be in bed, she was under the doctor but that it was her duty to keep going and she proposed to do that until such time as her Lord chose to take her, which, as things were going, would not be long now. She said she had one gentleman at the back and one upstairs and this room was taken by Mr. Yenish but she hadn't had a penny for it since the first week; there was eleven weeks rent owing and she hoped she would get it . . . or else. However, Mr. er must understand that there was no ill will, no ill will at all but she was a working woman; letting rooms to the young gentlemen was her livelihood and it stood to reason . . . etc., etc., etc. Furthermore, there had been a Turkish gentleman came shortly after Mr. Yenish had left, asking for him, she hadn't been able to tell him nothing about where Mr. Yenish was and he'd left without offering to pay a penny piece! It stood to reason, she said, that no one, no matter who they were, could go on indefinitely. Mr. Yenish had left all his luggage, there it was, piled in that corner just as he'd left it, and there would come a time when she would be forced, but forced, to get rid of the luggage for what it was worth, to cover herself that is. No one could go on indefinitely as things were, it stood to reason . . .

Nuri bey had some difficulty in following her, she repeated herself a great deal and used expressions which, good though his English was, were new to him. Finally he realised that what would really interest her was money and he ostentatiously brought out his notecase and toyed with it.

He was right; she changed down at once into a lower gear.

"To what extent is my young friend in your debt to date?" Nuri bey asked.

"Well, sir, it's eight weeks of last term and nearly three of this at five pounds a week."

"I see," but Nuri bey did not see at all. "But as he has had no meals?"

"Meals! That doesn't include meals. Bed, the room and use of bathroom. They pay for their own electric heating with a meter, they bring their own sheets and the laundry is extra; of course, I shouldn't think of charging for that, seeing as there wasn't any."

"That is kind," Nuri bey murmured gravely. "And you are able to live on this and the amount you get from the other two gentlemen?"

"Barely, barely." She folded her arms and looked out of the window at the grim, dirty grey-brick houses across the road.

"I shall be pleased to give you a little over and above what we owe if you would oblige me by telling me all you know about Mr. Yenish's movements."

"Me? Well, I don't know very much, but anything I can do to help . . ."

"How long was he here?"

"Let me see now; it wasn't the whole week not by a long chalk. The first morning I came in to make his bed, it hadn't been slept in."

"And he did not start to unpack his luggage?"

"I don't think so. See, it's still strapped up. He went to his college and brought back a suitcaseful of these books which he put on these shelves." She pointed out an empty cheap fibre case which Nuri bey looked at carefully. He opened it and looked inside, lowering his head and sniffing, much to her surprise; he closed it quickly.

"And I have an idea he's got a hand case with night things, what he had with him on the journey because it's not amongst this lot, as I can see."

"And did anyone come to visit him during the short period he was here?"

"I don't know. The gentlemen have their own keys and they go in and out as they like. I don't take no notice as a rule, it's only when I begin to suspect something I start worrying. I'm responsible to the Dean for what goes on; we've got to keep certain hours and we don't allow females in after eight, but the first few days of the Autumn term I don't worry too much. I tell them the rules and I expect them to keep to them—if they don't . . . they're out. Mine is a very respectable house . . ." etc., etc., etc.

Nuri bey arranged to pay her the money owing to date and up to the end of the term; she tried hard to conceal her pleasure but Nuri bey assured her that she had not seen the last of him, he would call from time to time to see if anything had happened with regard to Mr. Yenish. It was even possible that the young man would return either for good or for some of his possessions. "If he does," Nuri bey said, "he is to get in touch at once with the college authorities. You can tell him that his father has died suddenly. You can also tell him that I called, I am an old friend of the family." He gave her his name and address in St. Giles. "He should be able to find me here." Then he carefully counted out the requisite number of five-pound notes and gave them to her.

"What about the other young men in the house?"

"Mr. Yenish doesn't know them; they're at another college; they've probably never met. What a terrible thing, Mr. Yenish going off like that! I do hope nothing has happened to him."

"Do you?" Nuri bey looked at her, a long speculative look. "So do I."

"Well, good-bye, Mr. er, it's been a pleasure." And as he left she said: "What was that name you called me when you came?"

"Just my bad English, I'm afraid."

"Well, I never! It sounded just like Oxmarm, and I thought that a bit of cheek, really I did!" He thought she might possibly be smiling but as her hand was covering her mouth he couldn't be sure.

> . . . and finally, my dear Landrake, this evening I went to a restaurant where, Mr. Harp told me, the Lefties (as he calls

them) gather in the evenings. I was not disappointed. Ten or more of them were there and as I ate my meal I observed them closely. Though there was a variety of dress I noted a certain similarity in them all which would mark them at once as members of that particular group. None were clean, all had long hair, all slouched or slumped and all wore expressions which I cannot describe in English, but the nearest I can get to it is discontented. They sat round the two tables, my dear friend, and spoke not a word. In time they were joined by two others in the course of an argument; this argument went on for a long time, both were talking together, neither was listening to the other and occasionally one would thump the table so that the china jumped up and down. I could not understand what they were saying though it was loud enough at times. There were no girls amongst them though the length of their hair made one think at first sight, that one or two of them were women. Each generation has its group of young decadents; I understand that a writer called A. J. A. Symons has described the word ". . . a spiritual and moral perversity." We have no similar group in Turkey but I see that in a people of such varied characteristics as yours a growth of such young people is inevitable. Let them be perverse, my friend; *why not*?

I await anxiously your reply to my last letter; though the eagles may be here I trust I shall find no carcase.

Nuri

On the morning of the fourth day, Nuri bey shot out into St. Giles and turned towards the Randolph. He had not taken more than forty paces when a girl riding a bicycle on the other side of the road dismounted and came across, wheeling her machine. It was Hannah Benson and, as he watched her approaching with a slight smile, Nuri bey's heart turned; she was so like a girl he once knew called Jenny, who had kissed him.

"I've been looking for you," she said, shifting the load of books she was carrying from under her arm to the saddle of her bicycle. "I'm afraid I was rather a beast the night before last when you called. I'm sorry."

Nuri bey smiled his thin smile as though he had known it all along. He bowed. "I accept your apology," he said formally, "it is okay. May I walk with you if you are going somewhere?"

"To a lecture, but not to worry; it is more important to talk to you."

She must have changed her mind about him because, whereas at their first meeting she said nothing, she now talked a great deal, the main gist of it all being that she could not really believe that Jason had walked out on her without a word of explanation. Sometimes, she said, she was so miserable and bewildered that she could hardly be civil to anyone. And at other times she felt that Jason was in some kind of bad trouble and must be helped. She asked Nuri bey how well he had known him and he told her that he was a friend of the family who had seen Jason from time to time, perhaps a dozen or so times a year, ever since he was an infant. He had formed the opinion that he was a "very nice boy" but could say nothing beyond that as they had never been on intimate terms.

It was half an hour and they were down in Christ Church meadow before she came to the point round which she had been directing a course: the girl Ronda.

". . . and I'm absolutely certain he wasn't attracted to her, in *that* way; it was just that . . ."

"Yes, my dear?"

"Just that . . ." She burst into tears and Nuri bey was so embarrassed that he did what turned out to be the best thing, he pretended not to notice and she soon recovered; sympathy begets more and more tears, which would not have been seemly whilst walking with a middle-aged man in Christ Church meadow.

"And so it seems to you that for both Jason and the girl to disappear at the same time must mean that they are together?"

"I'm not sure that they did disappear at the same time, I don't know anything about the girl's life, I only know that she hasn't been seen since the beginning of last term and I haven't found anyone who can say they actually saw her then. All I know is that she hasn't been around. Jason used to talk to me about her."

"He did?"

"He was interested in everything and everybody and, if she didn't have this appalling fascination for some undergraduates, I wouldn't have given it a thought. About the last baby she had there was a collection; they sent the hat round to give her enough money to go abroad. They got the fare to somewhere for her but she was back before you could say knife, as pregnant as could be and seen sobbing against the wall one evening in Long Wall street by lots of people. They say she often goes into Latimer but the Dean runs like a hunted stag in the opposite direction when he sees her coming." She giggled a little and Nuri bey was comforted to see that she had managed to cheer herself up. He encouraged her:

"And what do you think Jason would do with this girl?"

"He'd do something mad like marry her out of pity."

"He won't have done that; there wouldn't be any need to disappear if that is what happened."

They turned round and walked back the way they had come in silence which Nuri bey broke at last by saying: "There is more than one problem: my friend Landrake in Turkey acts strangely; the Yenish father is killed and at present no one knows by whom; the Yenish son has disappeared but the father knew sometime before he was killed and did nothing; I myself have been followed from Turkey by a man who, I believe, came to look for Jason before Christmas." Nuri bey stopped and looked round. "I have not seen him since the day before yesterday and my new problem is *where is he*? I am of the opinion that all these problems are but one and when I shall shortly find the answer it will cover the questions I have just outlined to you."

"Shortly!" Hannah exclaimed, eyes wide.

He modified it to: "In a few days. It must be so because time is not on our side. I must find that young man quickly." He beat his fist into the palm of his other hand. "It is essential to get him back to his studies so that he may sit for his exams in the summer and get a First Class degree."

"Bravo!"

"Keep in touch with me, Miss Hannah Benson, and look out for a man so high, dressed in black with a black felt hat, square shoulders, more square than your men are now wearing, and toes like this." Nuri bey turned his toes slightly inwards. "He walks like a swan but in no other way does he resemble that graceful bird."

She did not kiss him, like the other young lady had done but she squeezed both his hands warmly with one of hers, jumped on her bicycle and rode up High Street, with a wave.

Nuri bey stood on the edge of the pavement, staring down into the gutter whilst the traffic passed, missing him by inches. He was thinking of a French film he had seen long ago which had haunted him; a man determined on revenge, followed another out into the wilderness; they walked and walked, one after the other; out in the Jordanian desert they walked and always the small black figure, square and determined, was a hundred yards or so behind the pursued. On they went, throwing off parts of their city clothes, wiping the sweat out of their eyes; completely lost, on and on they struggled through grilling heat until Nuri bey writhed in his seat with anxiety, and soon, with a singing in his ears and a throbbing in his head, he watched the pursuer catch up with the pursued, drag him along still hopelessly lost and, in the end, each helped the other to destruction; the two men lay dead on the rocks with the blazing sky above them in which the vultures circled. And, come to think of it, his pursuer was like the one in the film, the black hat, the tiny moustache, the full, stupid eyes. He looked round, half expecting to see him lurking about the entrance to the meadows.

A few minutes later in the bank he asked to see the manager, telling him that he was seeking a young Turkish client of theirs whose father had died suddenly in tragic circumstances and asking if the manager could give him any information about Jason Yenish. But the manager was not entirely satisfied; another man, said to be a Turk, had called before Christmas to ask for information and he had not been given any. The police, too, had made enquiries. Nuri bey pointed out that naturally the bank would not give information with regard to a client's affairs if everything were as it should be. But, as it was, that client had now been missing some eleven weeks, surely it was now time to speak to an old friend of the family who had been sent by that family to make enquiries.

But still the manager was not satisfied and Nuri bey was obliged to tell him details of Torgüt Yenish's death. "The father was murdered and I have reason to suspect that they are looking for the son to murder him in the same manner," he said finally. The manager examined Nuri bey's passport, gave him a long and searching look and reluctantly told him that Jason Yenish had come into the bank and had taken out all the money which had been paid in for the term's expenses; that is, one hundred and sixty pounds.

"I advised him not to do this," the manager said, "but he told me it was absolutely necessary. I was under no illusions that the money would be usefully spent but, as the young man has not so far had any money difficulties, I could hardly refuse. He took the money away in cash."

"Ah!" Nuri bey felt refreshed, as though he were at last getting somewhere.

"Since then we have neither heard nor seen anything of him."

As he left the manager suggested that he go to see an elderly relative of Yenish's mother, Lady Mercia Mossop: "Quite a character," he said, "as old as the hills and a lot more eccentric but I do know she was fond of the boy. I haven't seen her since her sister died recently because she's had to get rid of the fearful old car they had; she couldn't afford to have it maintained any more and the thing just seized up one morning and refused to move." He laughed a little. "Poor old dear, she'll be terribly upset about Yenish, though, incidentally, I wonder if anyone has told her he's . . . vamoosed."

"I shall tell her," Nuri bey decided.

"But go carefully; she's so old, a strong breath of wind would blow her over, and a shock might kill her."

6

The omnibus he required to take for Coverley Court was standing empty at the bus station and not due to leave for another quarter of an hour; he had time for coffee and a sandwich at the café in the bus yard. As he stood at the counter, Nuri bey allowed his gaze to range round and before long he saw what he wanted to see; the dark beetle-like figure of Arnika, standing in the far corner of the bus yard; this time he was wearing sun glasses. Without hurrying, Nuri bey finished his sandwich, ordered and drank another cup of coffee and sauntered across past his bus which was now filling with passengers.

"Still at it, my compatriot. I should give it up; you will not get the information you require." There was a long pause. "You are following me," Nuri bey said precisely, "because you think you will then discover the whereabouts of young Yenish. You are wrong, my man. He has left the country."

"I do not think so," Arnika returned.

"But yes, I assure you," Nuri bey said confidentially. "Furthermore, Arnika, I have reported you to the authorities."

"What authorities?"

Nuri bey gave his most mysterious Eastern smile, thin lipped, not kind. "The Special Branch." Though incorrect and untrue, it sounded splendidly authentic in Turkish. "The department that looks after the importation of drugs to this country. The Vice Squad," he added in English.

Arnika's face darkened.

"You see," Nuri bey explained lightly, reverting to Turkish, "I have had but one adventure in my life and it was in connection with the exporting from my country of the raw material of drugs, opium compressed into blocks which can quite simply be converted into heroin pills. Heroin, *the white stuff*, they call it, which can be quickly dissolved, drawn into a syringe and plunged into a young arm, or even an old one for that matter. It is a thing I, unfortunately, have cause to know something about. In the words of a good friend, the trading in such material is the one *unforgivable sin.* I have seen someone in the last stages . . ."

People were standing near them, Nuri bey grasped Arnika's arm and led him across the road into the shadow of Worcester College wall.

". . . and it is something unforgettable. In the end they go to skin and bone and all they do is to think how to pay for the next shot; they'd sell anything down to their mother's eyeglasses and their father's false teeth for the gold; they lose all self-respect; they lie and steal; they'd even steal dogs to make a few shillings; they sob and scream with terror at nothing; they suffer tortures of stomach-pain; they retch and gibber; they can't eat, can't sleep; they get mad fits and break up the place; and, right at the last, if they do manage to get their shot, it doesn't have any effect." They were pacing up and down outside the gates of Worcester College but no one took any notice; the sight of someone pouring out their whole soul in passionate appeal to another is no strange one in those ancient precincts. Nuri bey stopped and put both his arms on the shoulders of the shorter man:

"I tell you," he said, "there's nothing stronger in the whole wide world than the craving for drugs; they know they'll die in agony but they don't care; they lie about anywhere, in bed or on a pile of sacks, they do not have any will left, they rot to death."

Arnika, staring fascinated up through his dark glasses into Nuri bey's great burning eyes, was uncomfortable; he shrugged himself aside but there was no getting away.

Nuri bey went on: "For a European who cannot take drugs in moderation as they do in the East, it is the uttermost of degradation. Half the crime that is committed is caused by drugs and the United Nations are insisting that the penalties for drug peddling be ruthless."

They paced again, side by side.

"Have you nothing to say? We know that you are connected with an opium plantation; we know, in fact, where it is, we know that you have a machine for compressing it into blocks, and we know a good deal about the arrangements you make to get it out of Turkey. We know that from a small quantity of opium one can easily produce heroin to the value of thousands of pounds . . . we also know that a man must live, but not that way, not that way."

There was a sickly sneer on Arnika's face.

"I am no murderer," Nuri bey went on, "but if I see you around much more, I shall have to kill you, as a soldier shoots a soldier of the enemy side, because you are an enemy of the world, mankind's enemy."

Subdued by the power of his own argument, Nuri bey stopped and stared at Arnika; he had meant what he said and was deeply impressed by it. So was Arnika: he was always the colour of lard, now he was the colour of rancid lard, the flaws in his skin showing up like specks of growing mould.

"I can guess now, because it has all happened before: Torgüt Yenish was one of the ring, is it not so?" Arnika continued to say nothing. "The son also?" No reply. "I can tell you that it is of no use to follow the son; you will never recover the opium blocks he brought over to England with him."

Arnika jumped as though he had been pricked with a large needle. "Where is it?" he croaked.

"Sold," Nuri bey extemporised triumphantly. "For about four thousand pounds, cash."

"Where?"

"In the usual sources."

"But it was stolen!" Arnika shouted. "It did not belong to young Yenish, the thief!"

"I could return to you the case in which the opium was packed," Nuri bey suggested comfortably. "At present it is empty of opium but full of smell, a sour vegetable smell, recognisable anywhere."

"The woman, that woman!" Arnika clenched his fist and spoke through closed teeth. "Everything has run smoothly for years but at last the woman has discovered all, the confounded foreigner! She hated her husband and she did this thing out of revenge. Allah! She killed her husband and she shall in her turn be killed."

Nuri bey did not blench easily, he was the colour of a hazel nut anyway: now he went a slightly more silvery shade.

"The Yenish woman," he murmured casually.

Arnika did not answer, but neither did he contradict; absently he was biting his fingers. Nuri bey, too, was mentally biting his nails; it was one thing to tell Arnika that Jason had left the country but quite another to cause Arnika to fly back to Istanbul, to the great peril of Tamara. He had to do some quick thinking.

"I am not convinced," he said at last, "that young Yenish has left this country yet. He has all that money on him and he clearly cannot bank it here either under his own name or any other, it is too large a sum for a young man to bank without some enquiries taking place."

"It has been reported to me," Arnika said, "that young Yenish was seen in London." He made a kind of grimace which seemed to be a particularly unpleasant smile. "He was collecting a ration of heroin such as is allowed in this country to regular addicts."

Nuri bey felt a great physical nausea begin to sweep over him; he resisted it and succeeded in looking unimpressed.

"Impossible," he snapped.

Arnika, renewed by something he had thought, flashed out at him: "Nuri the lion they called you two years ago when Miasma was drowned and the eunuch hanged; they said you were as strong as a lion and as cunning as a fox. Now you are trying your famous cunning upon me but I am not deceived. Torgüt bey may be dead but all is not fled save gall."

He turned and strutted away, swan-toed and somehow inevitable, sure-to-happen. Nuri bey, unseeing, wandered through the quad and out into the garden, as quiet and ancient as that of Latimer. He sat on a seat, seeing nothing, thinking hard. At last he jumped to his feet and literally ran through the quad into the street and hailed a taxi standing at the taxi office near the bus station for the bus had long since left.

Coverley Court was approached by a drive in appalling condition. For nearly a mile it wound up between cultivated fields; an old sheep track, a series of bends and twists to the plateau on which the house had been built some three hundred years ago. There was a huge cypress tree, mullioned windows, a magnolia tree with its shiny green leaves trained against the golden stone walls, sharp-angled gables to hold the heavy stone-roofing and an air of smiling, happy decay about the whole place. The front door stood wide open and a minute dog, like a small dust-sausage, tangled and unkempt, tore out and tried to savage his shoes, making a great deal of noise. Presently, round the side of the house, came an enormously tall old woman wearing brown corduroy slacks, tied with twine at the knee, and wheeling a barrow-load of horse-manure; her hair was a grey mop and her face was by no means handsome but she was what Nuri bey was gradually learning to call "nice." That is, she smiled, something the English do too easily but which usually draws a response from a foreigner.

"Down Fido!" she shouted once or twice. "Isn't it splendid, you have now actually met a dog called Fido! We call them all by that name; there have been Fido Mossops here since the First Fido ever. Can I help you?"

"Surely, it is better that I help you," Nuri bey suggested.

"You could help me," she returned, "to shovel this muck to the bottom of our magnolia there, but not in that nice suit. It can wait. Now, what do you want?"

When Nuri bey told her, she said it was not a question which she could answer easily and together they went through the house, into the kitchen, and she banged a kettle on to the gas cooker, saying she would make a pot of tea.

"You know, we're funny old die-hards here; we haven't got electricity, would you believe it? My grandfather was a pioneer of gas and started a gas undertaking for the little town of Coverley which is two miles from here. He had the gas pipes brought up through the fields but when it came to having electricity, after the last war, Miranda and I simply couldn't afford the enormous sum they wanted for bringing it up underground. Neither could we bear the idea of ugly posts striding across our glorious view and the garden, so we've had all the gas brackets for light removed and we simply use oil lamps, which are a fearful nuisance, and candles. We miss having television, of course. But if you come to England as a foreign visitor it is essential, amongst the sights, to number an eccentric or so, and I suppose I'm one."

Whilst she talked she spent some time rattling about with innumerable tins, opening and shutting them and at last brought out some cake, which she put down on the kitchen table on a plate. She also found two thick pottery mugs, sugar in its packet and milk in its bottle. Oddly enough, Nuri bey did not doubt for a single moment that she was Lady Mercia Mossop; he had sometimes seen old ladies of the kind striding energetically up and down Istanbul's hilly streets and always they behaved as though they owned the place. The Mothers of Warriors, he called them to himself, or ought to be, but he understood about the whole ferocious war that had killed off their men; he had seen some of their graves, in lines of hundreds, at Eceabat near the Dardanelles, carefully tended by Turkish women, and had read the carved words that "Their Name Liveth Forever" on the stone.

"No milk, no milk for Mr. Iskirlak!" she sang out happily.

"My friends call me Nuri bey."

"Nuri bey, Nuri bey!" She poured boiling water into the brown teapot. "I feel we shall have much to say to each other, Nuri bey." She shut the kitchen door and the back door and sat down at the table. "Now, tell me, who has sent you to look for Jason Yenish? Why have you come here?"

He told her some of the story; the father had died suddenly, the mother had asked him to come, the boy had not been heard of since the beginning of the Michaelmas term. She listened with great attention.

"But have you seen the boy?" Nuri asked earnestly.

"I have a great affection for that boy," she said evasively. "Will you have some cake?" It was no time for eating cake but Nuri bey helped himself, he felt he needed sustaining. "His grandmother was our younger sister; my sister, Miranda and I, were amused by her in the way girls are by one who is so much younger than themselves. She wasn't one to sit at home waiting for a husband to turn up, as Miranda and I did, to our great detriment; she was full of the spirit of adventure and when, staying with friends in London, she met a Russian nobleman who asked her to go back to Russia for a winter to teach English to his young daughters, she leaped at it. It wasn't quite The Thing, you know, but our parents were not bound by convention and they didn't have an awful lot of money. They let her go, and how we envied her! I can remember Miranda and myself trying to help her pack, looking with admiration at all the new clothes she and Mamma bought for her in London. Then off she went with Miranda and me standing on the doorstep, this very front doorstep, and watching her drive away with Mamma and Papa, who were seeing her off in London.

"My dear, she was married within a year to a handsome Russian nobleman, a widower. It was like a fairy-story. Mamma and Papa went to St. Petersburg for the ceremony and it was promised that Miranda and I were to go the following year for our summer holiday, for three months."

She drank her now cooling tea in big gulps and, refreshed, she went on: "You know the rest. Her husband was in the army and was one of the first to be killed in the Revolution but I must say, he had made as good provision for his wife and baby as he could. Our parents were frantic with worry but darling Mamma was attacked with a serious illness, she was deadly ill for months and Papa sat, stricken, watching her die. He died himself the following winter from pneumonia they said, but we thought it was because he no longer wished to live without her. And our sister herself was not so very long-lived. Only we two old hobgoblins lived on, and on, and on, keeping the flag flying, or rather, keeping the weeds from growing. Miranda died this winter and I don't suppose it will be long before I follow, only, by God, I'll do it on my feet. I've got to keep the place decent for Jason, since the National Trust won't have it without a huge endowment."

Nuri bey started. "He may be dead."

She seemed undismayed by the thought. "The last, the very last of the Mossops," she said, "and I hope he'll change his name when he inherits."

"Dead," Nuri bey insisted, "what if he's dead?"

He felt a wave of irritation as she sat looking across at him, her arms folded on the bare scrubbed wood, her face tranquilly unworried. He was determined to shake her out of her complacency. "I said, he may be dead," he shouted. "The Yenish family have enemies." He remembered what the bank manager had said about her but simply did not believe it; she was no fragile old lady whom a strong breath of wind would blow over. He lowered his voice but spoke slowly and clearly: "Torgüt Yenish did not die naturally, he was shot dead last week in his study. No one was in the house but his wife. There are those who think Tamara killed him, including, I would not be surprised, the police."

But still she did not react and Nuri bey began to wonder if she was stone deaf or mentally defective.

"How do they know no one was in the house?" she asked. And after a long, long pause she said: "And if Tamara did kill him? He deserved it."

Nuri bey stared fascinated across the table. He added: "Because he was an enemy of the world?"

She nodded and, in the emotion of the moment, Nuri bey found himself clasping the gnarled and, it must be said, extremely dirty, old hand across the table.

After tea they went into the drawing-room, a beautiful room and one which was certainly lived in. An enormous sofa stood in front of the wide fireplace in which logs smouldered on a mountain of white ash. A long oak table behind the sofa bore bowls of sprouting bulbs; Nuri bey recognised them because tulips are Turkey's national flower. A lawn-mower, upside down on some newspapers, slowly dripped oil. She whisked the dog and a basket of raffia off the sofa before Nuri bey sat down and she herself sat in a wing-chair covered with rich gold velvet, shabby now and worn bare at the arms. There was a threadbare hearth rug but the rest of the floor was uncovered, a huge Aubusson carpet was partly draped over the grand piano; it was badly frayed and had a number of holes in it.

"Isn't it a pity," she said, "they want hundreds of pounds for repairing the carpet, so I'm just leaving it there to show we have, at least, got one." She gave a great gust of laughter. "Aren't I a *petite bourgeoise*!" She lighted a cigarette from a packet in her jacket pocket. "Now, Nuri bey," she said, "tell me, tell me absolutely everything, beginning at the beginning."

Nuri bey was always inclined to be cautious in his judgment of newly-met people; but caution did not enter into this acquaintanceship, he liked her as much as it is possible to like anyone on half an hour's knowledge of them. He did, in fact, tell her everything relevant, ending with: "And I should like to say that I love Tamara, I think perhaps I have always loved her, but now that it seems likely she loves me, my whole world has changed, she is my sun, moon and stars; if anything happens to her I shall go mad, and this is not the vainglorious boast of a young love-sick man."

She picked up a pair of shabby bellows with long handles and started to blow the fire into flames. "I believe you; you Turks don't do things by halves, especially when you are angry."

"You think that my idea that Tamara may be in danger is not exaggerated?"

"I am not sure because I cannot see how it will benefit this particular gang of dope-merchants to do away with the whole Yenish family of three."

Nuri bey sprang up, pushing the dog aside with his foot, and paced the room. "I cannot decide whether I should return to Istanbul and protect my beloved one or whether I should stay here and continue the search for her son. She says that life will hold no more joy for her if her son is dead. But what good will her son be to her if *she* is dead?"

"You're in a quandary," the old lady said from beside the fire, "heads they win, tails you lose." He did not know what she was talking about; he stared down at the upturned lawn-mower.

"Tamara doesn't want him home so much as, what did she call it? reinstated; she wants him back in his college working for his final exams."

There was a curious look on the old lady's face as she said: "Tamara is a mother and I am not; Tamara will have to learn that one cannot direct these young people; what she wishes for her child is not necessarily what he should have."

Nuri bey was astonished, he came across to her and sat on the sofa arm. "But the parents wishes are paramount," he said.

"Not at all, not at all! In your country, perhaps, but you are still half a century behind in the march of time, in spite of your absolutely detestable Atatürk . . ."

A sharp and stimulating argument ensued and ended in a completely non-rancorous deadlock. Lady Mercia rocked with laughter: "Oh, I like you, Nuri bey: you listen to people! But seriously, my friend, I love young people and I do not think we oldies know what is best for them always."

"Tamara is not old," Nuri bey put in quickly, "but surely to sit for an examination for which he has studied for three years is absolutely necessary?"

"There could be, mind I say *could be*, more important things. One's children must live their own lives the way they must live them, and if we see them doing the wrong thing and shout *stop*! they will not stop but go on, as we think, to their destruction. Sometimes we are right and sometimes we are wrong."

"So," Nuri bey said, bending his head in agreement. "Suppose there is a flaw in Jason's character, because the taking of drugs always arises from a flaw in the personality, so I believe. Must he not be saved from himself?"

She did not reply but took the crumpled packet from her pocket and lit another cigarette.

"Can you see him, quite demoralised, crawling about the floor on hands and knees looking in empty corners for *the white stuff*? Shouting for it, gibbering for it, banging his head against the wall for it; then lying anywhere, half-conscious . . . then the awful cramp, the screaming, the tears . . ."

"Stop, stop, that's *enough*! And anyway, that's all out of date. *The white stuff* is fearfully old hat, as they would say. Drugs are in a much more enticing form nowadays, all kinds of pills in fascinating and pretty colours; heart-shaped *Happy-pills*, tiny plastic capsules with varied-coloured grains inside. I've heard all about it from my dear Jason."

Nuri bey walked across to one of the great windows and looked out over the ha ha to the field where cows grazed.

"There's just one thing that is stronger to an addict than the wanting of the drug," she said.

"Yes, what is that?"

"I'm a bloody old woman, Nuri bey, but I'm not a sentimental one, and I'm not religious or anything like that but believe me, there's one thing greater than the longing for drugs and that is the longing for love; don't be sick, I don't mean sexual love, I mean a real affection, a belief in the essential good in the addict. It's the only thing that will do any good."

"Are you right? That Miss Smith, the probation officer I told you about; I ask myself if she would agree?"

"Ask her."

Nuri bey looked bewildered.

"Oh, go away, go away, Nuri bey. My head is splitting and I must think."

"I've upset you. I'm sorry," Nuri bey said, absolutely contrite.

"I'm getting too old to think but give me a day; come back to-morrow." And as he turned to go, she cried sharply: "You will, won't you?"

Fido saw him out, standing on the front portico and glaring after him through the fringe of hair which hung down over her eyes but through which she managed to see everything, even the merest unnatural twitch of a rhododendron leaf. With a wild cadenza of really unpleasant yapping she pelted in amongst the bushes and from the frantic noise she made she might easily have been tearing a sheep limb from limb. Nuri bey distinctly heard a Turkish oath and a shriek of anguish from Fido. With swift strides he hurried into the fray and caught the back of Arnika's overcoat, jacket and shirt collar in a comprehensive handful. Fido wasted no time in lamentation; she struggled round from lying winded on her back, on to her feet and set to work again at the turn-ups of Arnika's trousers.

Nuri bey brought his revolver out of his right-hand pocket; he intended to press the gun to Arnika's temple from behind and fire but something, somehow, stopped him. Later he was to wonder at the working of Kismet, if the wretched man had dropped dead in the shrubbery without knowing what had hit him, it would have been his nirvana in comparison to what actually did happen to him. It could only have been the intervention of Allah which prevented him from dying a beautifully simple death amongst Lady Mercia's rhododendrons.

Nuri bey dragged him out into the open and called himself a number of picturesque names; he ought not to have forgotten Arnika when he was sitting on the seat in Worcester College garden. Arnika had either followed him in a taxi, at least to the foot of the drive, or waited for the taxi to return to ask the driver to take him to where he had just driven the Turkish gentleman. He must remember that if you are being seriously followed, it is not a spasmodic thing but something that is with you always, even unto the end; which could have been this same minute, if Allah had willed it, which He had clearly not.

Fido bustled, only slightly wilted, back to the house; Nuri bey kept a firm hold on Arnika. "I am sick of you, Effendi, you are getting badly on my nerves, you are a headache. All I have said to you, is it of no avail?"

"You talk too much; you have told me a pack of lies, first you said Jason Yenish had left the country; then you are not so sure. You say he has sold the stuff but I think you lie, and lie, and I do not trust you, therefore I have to follow you. What are you doing here? Is Jason Yenish here?"

"Here?" Nuri bey smiled grimly and for a moment the idea passed through his head of asking Lady Mercia for the use of a wine cellar into which he could lock Arnika.

"I wish you no ill," Arnika whined, "I am but doing my duty. And my duty is to find the raw opium which has been stolen . . ."

"Stolen, ha! . . ."

". . . stolen, and I do not believe it is already sold; Jason Yenish would have no idea where to sell it. Those for whom it was intended in England have not received it and as they have already paid for half the consignment, it is essential that it be returned. If I cannot get it back I shall have to return to Turkey without it and my . . . my firm will then destroy the Yenish woman because she will inform the authorities against us."

Still holding his gun against Arnika's side, Nuri bey was in a strong position. "Why did you shoot Torgüt Yenish?"

"We did not. His wife shot him."

Frisking him, Nuri bey sadly removed a gun from his overcoat pocket.

"This is the second gun I have had to take but I shall give it back to you as I cannot carry two guns and you will assuredly buy another. I will give you an address that I have been given in London where Jason Yenish has, at least, spent some time recently. I am afraid your informant is only too right that the young man has been seen buying heroin in a London chemist. Whether you will find him in London or not, I do not know. What I do know is that I am going to ring for a taxi to come and fetch us both. We shall go to Oxford station and I will stay beside you until you are in the express train to London; thus I shall have time to call on my various friends in Oxford without having you come too."

He saw Lady Mercia looking through the window and signalled to her; when she came to the door, he asked her to ring for a taxi, saying that they would wait for it at the bottom of the drive. A splendid accomplice, she did not stop to ask questions but hurried to do as she was told. Whilst they took the long walk down the drive Nuri bey had time to make up a London address which he wrote on a piece of paper and gave to Arnika, together with the gun.

There was an hour to wait before the London train but when it was actually standing in the station and about to leave, Nuri bey, holding his gun and assuring Arnika that he would fire in this public place, if not to kill at least to draw attention to themselves, if he did not hand over his passport before leaving. Arnika backed towards the open door of the corridor carriage, Nuri bey following him hand in pocket. Arnika, still facing Nuri bey, took two steps up into the train.

"Hurry, I want your passport!" Nuri bey said.

Arnika undid his black overcoat and fumbled with things in his hip pocket.

Nuri bey brought out the gun: "Come on!"

Arnika looked down, sorting out his possessions and at the same time let out with his foot and kicked the gun from Nuri bey's hand; he actually laughed in Nuri bey's face as it fell down between the carriage and the platform: it was a wonderful revenge for the defeat in Blackwell's.

He slammed the door but Nuri bey, with a roar of anger, grabbed his tie and the front of his collar and shirt through the open window. Standing on the step, he put his face close to Arnika's and threatened him with strangulation if he did not hand over his passport. Unfortunately, the train started and two railway officials made a combined effort to drag Nuri bey off the moving train, which they succeeded in doing.

"We have to prevent people doing an injury to themselves, sir," one of them said apologetically and the other jumped down on the line, retrieved the gun and handed it to him. In spite of his anger, Nuri bey managed to give him half a crown.

The two officials looked at each other; knowing, as they did, that the travelling public consisted largely of lunatics and raving maniacs, they exchanged sardonic smiles.

Nuri bey walked into the gentlemen's lavatory and beat his forehead against the wall.

7

. . . and so, Landrake my dear, I must beg you to have the airport watched for the return of this *Sheytan* Arnika. I will repay you for the money it will cost you. If he returns it will be for the purpose of killing Tamara to keep her silent. The Turkish pashas, wishing to rid themselves of inconvenient persons, would send them to friends with a note saying: *on receipt of this please throw bearer in boiling oil.* I modify this however: the Bosphorus will do.

I hope you will understand the telegram I have sent off at once because, as soon as the *Sheytan* finds that the address I have given him for Jason is a fiction, he may fly to Istanbul at once and I trust you will already, as I write this, have someone on the watch.

As sure as the storks fly back to Eyup so will Arnika return to my city to destroy my beloved. Ah, my friend, this is no life for a middle-aged philosopher, I feel bewildered and inept but circumstances can make the man and I am learning rapidly, almost as quickly as my English improves!

Nuri

Tamara, my beloved,

Mashallah! how I need to see you again, to touch you, to be with you; it is six days since I saw you and already I wonder if you are but a moon-woman, made of moonlight, insubstantial as a dream; you are my heart-beats, my breath and my life itself, yet my arms are empty; food for the soul alone is, I have suddenly discovered, *not enough. Murram fi*, the Arabic for *I am in love*; ridiculous symbols for the glory in which I have walked for the past week.

Your Nuri

For a short time I had two guns; I hope you will keep yours always beside you ready for use.

Next morning, determined to find Probation Officer Smith, he waited for an hour and a half outside the Magistrate's Court. At last he saw her, with a sulky-looking boy, walking towards him. "May I speak to you a moment?"

"Yes, Mr. Iskirlak?" She smiled pleasantly but kept an eye on the boy. "Can I help you?"

She could help him; please could she tell him the address of Ronda's Oxmarm? She laughed: "Someone's been pulling your leg," she said. "If you mean Oxford landlady she doesn't quite come into that category though in fact she does let rooms, but not to undergraduates." Quickly she scribbled an address on an old envelope, wished him luck and hurried into the building with the sulky boy.

Nuri bey walked down a road under the railway bridge and, as he walked, went through less and less distinguished surroundings. He found the house and rang the bell. The woman who answered the door might as well have had a notice hung round her neck saying: "*Slattern, international type.*" She told him that Ronda had left her house some time ago. He said he knew that but could he have a few words with her. She said no, she was much too busy; besides, she'd spent long enough talking about that girl, least said soonest mended was what she always said. Her voice was so shrill that he felt like a sensitive glass that might at any moment shatter in pieces. He knew that, if he had waved a banknote in front of her, she might have invited him in but her whole manner was so objectionable that he hesitated.

"Go find her Aunty," the woman advised, "she'll tell you the lot."

"Anti?" Nuri bey was bewildered.

"Her Ma's sister; two streets away."

She gave the name and the number and he departed with the slam of her door sounding loudly the length of the street.

The Aunty lived in a neat bungalow called Holm Royd: a cheerful-looking place with many-coloured curtains in the windows and gay bunches of artificial flowers on the window sills, one bunch standing in a vase representing an Alsatian dog, the flowers sprouting from a hole in the back. He rang the bell, which startled him by giving out a three-note chime.

She was a colourful woman to whom he would have found it difficult to attach any label; she had red hair elaborately curled and piled up high, a red face of a different hue from the hair, and wore a cheerful expression; her figure was pressed into splendid foundations; altogether she formed the Turkish idea of womanhood-pattern, being far removed from the emaciated scraps of creatures that passed for women in England.

Nuri bey told her his name and his mission and she invited him in with welcoming noises.

"Sit down, dear, have a fag?" She took one herself.

"Anyone wants to talk to me about Ronda I've no objection, no objection at all; that poor kid has been on my mind since the minute she was conceived; if I could be sure what minute that was, there might have been some trouble saved because one of my husbands was in the running as father, at the time." She gave a great shout of laughter but nearly everything she said was lost on Nuri bey partly because he did not understand and partly because, as she sat down he was subjected to such an extraordinarily comprehensive view of those parts of the female which are usually hidden from sight, that his mind was not on what she was saying. He averted his eyes, however, and sat with the tips of his long fingers pressed together and his eyes on the illustrated wallpaper behind her gaudy head.

She stopped talking and waited for Nuri bey to give an account of himself, which he did, mentioning Jason Yenish by name. What he had to say, she evidently found satisfactory for she nodded: "That was one she called Jay, a foreign boy." She got up and, opening the cocktail cabinet, brought out a bottle of port and two glasses.

"You'll take a drop, Mr. whatever your name is, can't pronounce it!" she roared and Nuri bey was relieved that she was now perched on the arm of the sofa rather than sitting down. She did not need encouragement, she took much pleasure in pouring out the whole story.

Ada, that was her unfortunate sister, could do nothing with Ronda but then, with the life she led, it was hardly surprising. "Ada," she had often said, "take a warning from me, you're cutting a rod for your own back the way you carry on in the flat with that child around." But it was no good, Ada was . . . what she was, and poor little Ronda had been turned out after a flaming row.

"I was just between husbands then, dear, and up in Leeds, working in a gown shop to make it all ticketty boo for my decree nisi, so I was out of the picture. But when I got married and came back to Oxford (my husband's a manager at a car factory) I found Ronda living in a room with a friend . . . well, dear, they were nothing more nor less than a couple of common prostitutes. Then Ronda got ideas above her station, she got in with some of these college boys and she moved up in the social scale. For a time, when she had that first baby, a lovely little boy he was, (I'm childish meself so you can imagine how it broke my heart,) she was living in a house with a lot of those layabouts, beats. That poor kid! She had the undergraduates taking him out in the pram whilst she was off jumping into bed with another of their pals. They said they believed in Free Love. I says to her Free What, I says, don't come that Free Love on me! That house was a disgrace, I can tell you; the University authorities had it shut down but they moved on somewhere else until the authorities got wind of it and shut that down too."

She lighted another cigarette and poured out more port. "It was downhill all the way. Slimming pills started it, no, marihuana cigarettes first, that was after she got the little boy adopted, said she felt lost without him. And after that she went on *Purple hearts*, that's a kind of drug appeals to the young because of the sentimental name, well, I mean to say . . ." She spread her hands wide and looked hopelessly at Nuri bey. "The country'll do a lot for the unmarried mother with the first but the *second* time . . . you're on your own, believe me. This time she had the baby adopted before she even saw it, and they never showed it her; she signed it away at birth."

She sighed heavily. "And then she was on hard drugs before you could turn round, in pill form and heroin in a form you drink because the prick of an injection hurts them: they used to say it was, what did they call it? *non-addiction*? That means it doesn't become a habit but don't make me laugh! It becomes a habit all right. It's not like alcohol; with alcohol they're nice people when they're sober, like my poor second husband; he was an angel when he was sober, as true as I'm standing here, I adored that man. But my God, when he was drunk! But these drug-addicts: they do it for the kicks but what happens? When there's no more kicks out of it, they've *got to have it . . .*"

"I know, I know," Nuri bey said wearily, "I'm afraid I know all about it, madam."

"Yes, I can see it makes you tired like it makes me but what I can't understand is . . . how do they go on getting it? I've been to the police and I've talked to the probation officer and they tell me it's *all brought into the country illegal*!"

The port was beginning to give Nuri bey a headache; he was drinking much too early in the day.

"Please, madam," he begged, "help me to find your niece; I have reason to believe that she is with the young friend I mentioned and it is essential that I get in touch with him."

"I'll help you all I possibly can, as I said to the probation officer; poor woman, Ronda's driven her frantic. There's a warrant out for her for 'breach of probation order.' The shame of it all is driving me up the pole, mister, really it is."

Because he was hungry and because, when he had got used to her extraordinary way of talking she was good company, Nuri bey took her out to lunch. She drove him back into the city in her small car and, whilst she was parking it, Nuri bey went into the Randolph to secure a table. The man in the reception beckoned to him:

"Your friend, the Turkish gentleman, Mr. Arnika, has asked me to give you a message. I was to tell you he is back in town, sir."

"Back . . .!" he shouted, then controlled himself. "Is he here now?"

The receptionist peered round the hall. "I don't know, sir, maybe he will be in for lunch; shall I give him a message?"

Nuri bey was abstracted during luncheon but his companion, delighted with her surroundings, chattered away happily without seeming to notice his withdrawal. It was only with the coffee that she returned to the subject that interested him. "That young chap Jay, as she called him, had some aristocratic relations living not far from here in one of those big old houses you'd pay to see over. Two old dears, Ladies too . . . what was the name now . . . Moffat . . . Mowatt?"

"Mossop?"

"That's right. You've been to see them, have you?"

"There's only one now. Yes, I've been to see her and I must return to see her again to-day."

"Like me to run you out there? I've nothing doing this afternoon."

He could not think of anything against the idea and presently they were driving along the road the taxi had taken the previous day. It was a pleasant early spring day and Lady Mercia was found mowing the piece of lawn between the cypress tree and the ha ha. Fido, sitting erect under the tree, was watching her every move. The lawn mower was making a loud noise and she did not hear the arrival of Maisie's car. They got out and walked across to her and as she caught sight of them she jumped violently.

"Phew! You gave me a fright!" She turned off the engine and Nuri bey introduced Maisie as aunt of the girl Ronda. After the first words of greeting she asked Nuri bey if he would come into the house for a few moments. Leaving Maisie strolling about with Fido suspiciously at her heels, they went inside.

"Listen, Nuri bey. The Turk with whom you had your scuffle yesterday morning called on me this morning. I am most uneasy. He introduced himself in almost the same way that you did. He said he was a great friend of Torgüt Yenish, who had died suddenly, and that he wished to find his son to give him the news of his father's death."

Nuri bey beat his forehead with the front of his wrist. "I regret that I bring you nothing but trouble," he murmured, "I would have given much for this not to have happened."

"I'm sure he's a dangerous man, Nuri bey, a menace both to you and to my great-nephew. He does not mean well."

"He does not! But he wants information from us more than he wants our corpses, if that is any comfort . . ."

Though it was a pleasant morning, he was wearing his mackintosh, which he found useful in concealing the bulges in his jacket pockets, from which he felt a certain reassurance. He rubbed his hands. "At least Arnika is here and not on his way back to Istanbul at the moment, and I must confess that, though I fear him as much as you, I would rather have him here than there."

"Why have you brought the girl's aunt?"

"Because she was ready to bring me at once in her car and I also thought it might interest you to hear what she has to say about the girl."

"I'll go and talk to her now."

He nodded. "You can have her to yourself for a few minutes."

She knows something more than she tells, Nuri bey thought, she has an air of calm about her; if she had not seen Jason since he returned she would be more distressed: could she be concealing him here in this house? Glancing through the window he saw Maisie talking hard to Lady Mercia and very quickly he made a tour of the house. There were five bedrooms and a huge Edwardian bathroom on the first floor; he opened the door of each room and glanced inside. Lady Mercia's bedroom was clearly the only one occupied, the windows wide open, the bed made and covered with a piece of beautiful old embroidered velvet which he would like to have examined more closely, the big round table with a lamp beside the bed, telephone, a great many books and a vase of daffodils. All the other rooms had their curtains closely drawn, the windows shut and the beds covered with dust-sheets. The top floor had the same number of rooms but they were used as store rooms; one contained apple racks, another a carpenter's bench and tools ranged against the wall, and the rest were stacked with old furniture, pictures and trunks. There was another bathroom up here and Nuri bey looked at it carefully; the bath stood on great lion's feet, the taps were brass and had not been cleaned for years; he turned on a tap which moved stiffly and after a few hollow coughs a thin stream of rusty water appeared. Satisfied he sped downstairs and out on to the drive.

"Well, Mr. Nuri," Maisie cried, "Her Ladyship agrees with me that those two young people must be together, whatever else. If we find the one, we'll find the other and that's for sure."

Nuri bey made no reply because there seemed nothing adequate to say. The lawn mower stood silent, he pushed it gently, it seemed an immense weight for an old lady.

"The motor drives the blades," she volunteered, "but what I'd dearly love would be the sort that runs away with you."

"No gardener?"

"He died last year; he was only seventy-eight but he never really got over last winter. I've got a man who comes to-morrow, once a week now; I think my poor sister killed herself with overwork after our gardener died."

"How did you get this lawn mower out of your drawing-room and down the front steps?" Nuri bey asked thoughtfully.

"Ha ha! The postman!" She tapped Nuri bey's shoulder and gave another abandoned laugh. Though he looked pleasant, Nuri bey did not join in the laughter. He brought Arnika's revolver out of his pocket. "I would like to give you this."

"Oh, my goodness me!"

"It is loaded; there are five bullets in it. This is the safety catch. You fire it like this." He raised his arm and holding it at full length, fired the revolver across the ha ha and into the field. The gun gave a back kick which jolted his arm severely, Maisie screamed, Fido barked hysterically. "You see, you must be careful of the recoil, it could hurt you very much." One or two of the cows threw up their heads and tails and frisked about with wildly swinging udders.

"Take care, take care!" Lady Mercia cried. Aiming cautiously at nothing Nuri bey fired again and this time it worked. Maisie screamed even more piercingly than before, Lady Mercia held her face in her hands, and Jason came running round the side of the house.

Nuri bey took out his pocket handkerchief and wiped the gun lovingly. "Come here, Jason," he called. "I would rather you had this pistol than your aunt . . . it is a heavy thing for a lady!" He put both his arms on Jason's shoulders and, in the Turkish manner, kissed him on first one cheek and then the other.

8

The way he got Maisie off the scene was a miracle of tact; with nothing further said, he swept her into her little car.

"Quickly, quickly!" he urged, climbing in and slamming the door.

She started up, then, lowering the driving window, she leaned out, calling: "Bye bye, Lady Mossop, bye bye, dear!" and drove away. "What was all that about? Don't tell me that was the young fellow you're looking for? Why in such a hurry to get away?"

"Because," Nuri bey explained, "I am not a man on my own, I am haunted, shadowed. 'A bundle of nerves' is the English idiom, is it not? You have never been followed, wait till you are and you will understand. I came gladly in your car because I felt that he was less likely to follow us, but he was at Coverley this morning and for all I know he may still be around, not too near the house, perhaps, because of our little friend Fido. But the shots brought Jason out of his hiding place and I was afraid they might also have brought Arnika. So there was great need for haste, Mrs. Maisie!"

But as they drove back to Oxford he felt extremely worried. Whilst they had had lunch he had watched for and hoped to see Arnika, the *sheytan* would have been puzzled beyond endurance as to who Maisie might be. Now he was in a frenzy of anxiety lest Arnika had stayed at Coverley Court, wandering about in the vicinity, waiting to see whether Nuri bey turned up during the afternoon or not. If he had stayed he would have been well rewarded. Those who shadowed other people always seemed to have an unfair amount of success, and Arnika seemed to have the patience of a sphinx.

Nuri bey said good-bye to Maisie, who had clearly had the time of her life and waved cheerfully as she drew away down Queen Street. At the post office there were two letters:

Nuri my friend,
Your letter gave me great pleasure even though I was shocked and distressed that Arnika is on your heels. This is a man with whom Yenish had a lifelong partnership in guilt but I have always thought he was the sleeping partner. It seems now that he is far from sleeping and has done a good job of work. As he would not associate you with Yenish he must have followed Tamara when she came to see you . . .

Nuri bey remembered standing at the door of his house with Tamara as she was leaving, he could hear Tamara telling him about the stars and he heard himself saying confidently that he would leave immediately, ". . . to Yesilkoy by ordinary bus and wait at the airport for the next plane to Athens, or Rome and go on from there to London." A clear, starry night, his voice would have carried, the watcher would have heard every word.

. . . I have never actually met him but I have often seen him with Yenish at restaurants and on every occasion Yenish simply waved across to me and did not make any attempt to speak. Twice I saw him leaving Yenish's house as I arrived. He is a man I remember as walking with both hands in his pockets, almost a dummy figure and capable of anything. I shall at once find out more about him. Take care, old chum, for all our sakes. And good luck!

Landrake

Nuri, my darling,
I have never received a letter like yours nor can I write like you but thank you for it, it has made me so happy. I am watching Jupiter for you, he is still in your sign of Sagittarius but I am anxious about the new moon which may bring a change for the worse in your luck, dear heart. The police are still with me but Landrake is pleased, he says whilst the police are here I am safe, the house is being watched day and night, but who are

they hoping will come? The dog which returns to its vomit? At night I stand on the roof and know that the whole great canopy covered with stars covers you too, and, I pray, Jason. With love

Yours,
Tamara

With infinite pleasure, Nuri bey sent his telegram: JASON IS ALIVE AND WELL, NURI.

Yes . . . but!

Yes, *but*?

Nuri bey wrung his hands as he paced the thin carpet of his hotel bedroom.

Because the situation was extremely serious, Lady Mercia, in answer to Nuri bey's urgent telephone call, changed into her best, her second best, her third best, in fact, her only suit, scrubbed her hands, crammed a genuine Henry Heath felt hat with a kingfisher feather in the ribbon, on her head, telephoned for a taxi and travelled into Oxford for tea at the Randolph. He had chosen that hotel in the hope of seeing Arnika coming in or out.

She was delighted to be there and looked round her with appreciation. "Ages since I've been there. Have you ever wondered exactly *what* Randolph?"

He had not: he leaned forward anxiously. "And tell me, please, the girl Ronda is with Jason?"

She nodded. "In my old gardener's cottage beyond the stable yard, hidden from sight because it is so hideous. But there are two bedrooms, Nuri bey, and I honestly think they occupy one each. I order their food from my tradespeople and Jason pays me. He does the cooking and the housework. The situation is one which I find singular beyond belief. Nothing like that happened when we were young: everything was less complicated."

"What does she do with herself all day?"

There was a long pause whilst the waiter brought a laden tray; she poured out the tea and bit appreciatively into a cucumber sandwich.

"She . . . well, she reads innumerable paper-back romances costing about ninepence each which Jason buys for her from the village shop. She talks a lot, she's always talking. She cries a good bit, too. They have hysterical scenes to break up the boredom of it; she screams the place down; fortunately there isn't anyone but me within earshot. She hits him and they have struggles, once the table got knocked over and some pottery broken. Then she lies on her bed and sulks for hours at a time. I told you the old shot with the syringe was quite finished with, giving themselves injections frightens them. Jason said it started with a slimming drug in pill form she took when she was fifteen; I believe it has recently been made illegal but when I asked her about it she boasted that she'd 'always taken drugs, *of course*!' So Jason goes to London about once a fortnight, on an early train so that he won't meet anyone he knows, to buy her what they call 'heroin jam' of which he allows her a spoonful at a time, not more; he says, poor deluded boy, that he is giving her a fraction less every time."

"And he really believes he is curing her?"

"Yes, he does. Tell me, Nuri bey, what was his father like?"

Nuri bey made a wry face: "My friend Landrake tells me that I am incurious, that I accept people as I find them, that I like books more than people and perhaps he is right. Though I have known Torgüt Yenish many years I do not feel capable of describing, or explaining him to you."

"I met him, long ago when my sister and I went to Istanbul to see dear Tamara. I thought him a withdrawn man, someone living inside himself. But above all a man absolutely implacable."

"Implacable?"

"A man not to be appeased. Am I right?"

Nuri bey shrugged.

She went on: "I find Jason has this quality about him. Nor is he one to be either persuaded or dissuaded. He is not unintelligent; he must know that this girl is ruining him, that staying with her means that he will never pass his finals, that she is an absolute no-good and all the rest of it. He understands all that but still he is convinced that he must stay with her, 'rescue her from herself' he calls it. He has made a mission of it, he might well think he's been divinely appointed for the sole purpose."

She looked out of the window at the Martyrs' Memorial. "Those two, burned to death out there, had this same quality, call it what you like . . . the tiny proletarian name for it would be 'pig-headed' perhaps—it's the stuff that martyrs are made of but it's not very *useful*, is it?"

Nuri bey felt like banging the table with his fist but it was too crowded. "It is ridiculous!" he cried, over-loud so that a number of people sitting around in the thronged lounge having tea looked up in surprise. "In my country it could never happen."

"But as he is half Turkish, that is a foolish remark, if I may say so." There was a long pause whilst Nuri bey sat quietly fuming and Lady Mercia finished every last scrap of food on the tea tray.

"Nobody can do anything with that girl," she said when she had finished. "And never will."

Nuri bey told her everything that Miss Smith, the probation officer, had had to say.

"I agree with it all; I heartily detest the girl, though," and after another pause she added, "or do I?" She thought for a few moments: "What I feel about her is extremely complicated. I do detest her because, wherever she is, there is a small pocket of misrule; she will give pain and misery to everyone with whom she comes in contact, sooner or later, *but* the minute I can detach myself from what she is doing to Jason and indirectly to me, I can feel sorry for her. All the same, I know that the best thing to happen would be for her to fall off a roof and break her neck and she won't do that because there isn't an available roof."

Nuri bey stirred restlessly. "We do not advance," he stated soberly, "we have no plan of action. Speed is absolutely necessary, the matter is extremely urgent. I must return to Istanbul to report to his mother, who is gravely threatened with reprisals. We cannot waste time . . ." Once more his voice was raised to a shout.

"Sh . . . sh!" Lady Mercia looked round nervously. "People are looking at us. Keep calm, Nuri bey, we will think of something."

"Can you send Jason into Oxford to talk with me?"

She shook her head. "He cannot come."

Nuri bey marvelled that a young man like Jason should have asked for the help of an old woman. Now, drawing her chair closer to the table, she told Nuri bey everything, filling in the gaps in his own knowledge. Jason was a perfectly normal young man, returning from his long vacation at home in Istanbul to Oxford with a good deal of baggage on which he knew he would have to pay excess. His mother went to see him off, driving him to the airport in her car. His luggage was lifted out and carried into the Customs hall and he followed it, arranging to meet his mother at the lounge bar when she had parked her car and he had dealt with his baggage. He had two large suitcases, a duffle bag, his guitar case and a typewriter, all of which was weighed together and labelled. He paid the excess charge, left the baggage with the officer in charge, joined his mother in the bar for a drink, kissed her good-bye, left the lounge with his fellow passengers and boarded the plane. At Athens they changed planes, with a wait of half an hour. At London Airport he went through the immigration with everyone else and into the Customs hall where he saw his luggage standing on the bench. Another case had been added to it; it bore an identical passenger's baggage label and a label with his name and destination written in a handwriting similar to his own.

The Customs officer, extremely busy, was making his way along the bench towards him; uncertain, Jason waited.

"Is this all yours, sir?" the Customs officer asked and before Jason had made up his mind what to reply the Customs officer had made his own particular hieroglyphic in chalk on the six pieces and passed along. Jason looked round at the crowd, everyone intent upon their own business; except one man, a figure he recognised, dark glasses over eyes which sought his. Jason instantly picked up the pirate case. "Porter," he called. A porter swept his remaining five pieces on to the moving belt and Jason ran down the escalator to meet it below. He watched it packed into the back of the bus, tipped the porter liberally, jumped on the bus, stowed the suitcase under his seat before the bus conductor noticed and watched. It was only as the bus drew away from the exit doors that he saw the stocky black-clad figure standing in the background, watching the departure of the bus, hands in pockets, toes turned in.

Nuri bey nodded as though he already knew it all. "Amongst the porters at Yesilkoy there are certainly one or two paid to perform these necessary functions; the labels can easily be adjusted by someone actually handling the baggage."

"Yes, but they have to know in advance who is going. That is why Jason was sure his father had organised it."

"But he could at least have written to his mother during all these weeks," Nuri bey said reprovingly.

"This has all been a great shock to Jason; put yourself in his place. He learned at last what he had suspected for some time. And think of the cruel insolence of his father, putting him in the position of being actually found with the case of opium. If it hadn't been for sheer luck he could have been exposed and imprisoned. Was his father so harsh and cruel a man that he did not care at all?"

"No, no!" Nuri bey protested. "A young undergraduate returning to Oxford, surprised by the case which had been planted on him, surely he would never have been seriously suspected of deliberately smuggling. Much ingenuity goes into the exporting of the opium that they grow and they must take great risks. The idea was surely that Arnika should receive the case; as soon as the Customs officer had passed it he would have come up and taken it off the bench; only one in ten people would notice the label. No doubt it has worked many, many times. I, personally, would have taken no notice of a case which was not my own; I would certainly not have bothered to look at the label!"

"Well, there it is. I could not tell you when you came to see me yesterday. I could say nothing until I had spoken to Jason about you." She smiled: "Do you know what he said? 'A dreamy type who lives in a world of books; I've always suspected him half in love with my mother.' And when I questioned him further he said far from being a drug-peddlar your name had sounded from end to end of Turkey two years ago when you did what he called 'Fought a tough couple of drug-peddlars single-handed: got one drowned and the other hanged,' and he added that there were those who thought you shot a third."

Nuri bey looked grim. "It was not a joke," he said.

"Jason also said his father thought you the most astute man in Istanbul."

"No doubt why he asked me to search for his son. He must have known that it would not be long before I learned something of the truth!"

"But he was murdered, was he not? Was that to prevent him asking you to come and look for his son?"

"If it was, it was too late; he was dead within minutes of asking me!"

Lady Mercia leaned back in her chair. "Oh, dear, I'm tired," she said. "I can mow a lawn and dig over the vegetable garden without feeling it a bit but thinking about international drug smuggling, explaining it and worrying about Jason, I find absolutely exhausting. I suppose I've never been called upon to use my brain much."

She looked grey and very lined. The waiter took away the empty tea tray; people were leaving, the lounge was emptying.

"You are a wonderful old woman, we do not have them like you in Turkey, not a bit."

"Um."

"Soon I shall take you home in a taxi but first I shall ask for brandy for us both."

"That would be nice, dear Nuri bey, but we can't have one till six. But as a good Moslem, do you drink?"

"I am not a good Moslem but I do drink brandy, since the Prophet forbade only the drinking of *wine*." She laughed a little, then began to doze off. Nuri bey sat, his finger tips pressed together in a very characteristic attitude and watched the entrance door.

Two things seemed to him essential: to kill Arnika but to kill him cleverly so that no possible suspicion could be attached to him because, if it were, he would not be free to return to his beloved; and to remove, somehow, somewhere, the girl Ronda. Both were impossible; he was not a murderer nor yet an abducter; he was a philosopher, one who loves wisdom and knowledge, especially that which deals with ultimate reality, one who is serene, resigned. Such a one does not scheme to kill and to abduct.

But he would never remember that through his veins flowed a good strong stream of the wild rank blood of the Caucasus, of eagle-faced warriors, ones who flayed their enemies and used their skins for drums. They slashed themselves with their own swords, poured red hot ashes on their own heads and wailed themselves into morbid ecstasies. Nobody could call them nonentities.

Yet the grandson of one of these wild people now sat in the lounge of the Randolph Hotel in Oxford and tried to think of a neat clean way of confounding his enemies.

Lady Mercia was asleep, not with face fallen apart and hat askew, but sleeping tidily, like an effigy, with a faint smile upon her lips.

My dear Landrake,
This afternoon being Saturday and Arnika having vanished from the scene I have been to a football match and, my friend, I have never had a more exhilarating experience. The waitress from my hotel who, with her husband, is an aficionado, took me with them. I saw Oxford play against Manchester United competing for the final at which they win a silver cup. No sport could be more exciting; they played magnificently as a team, passing the ball from one to another with no one man trying to outplay another; smooth and precise and altogether glorious because so well-done; and the crowds, my friend, twenty thousand people roaring like one, and a small group of the opposition mad with joy when their side scored. This has nothing to do with my mission but it has much to do with my understanding and liking of the people of your country. Jason's elderly relative is talking to Jason and will telephone me when she has persuaded him to see me; I have not yet talked with Jason but at the present moment as I write I await a telephone call saying I can see him. I need not say I trust you are keeping the watch on the airport for Arnika. At the time of writing I believe he must have shot Yenish; though partners, I believe they were not friends.

Nuri

9

Jason was waiting for him in his elderly relative's drawing-room; he seemed neither sulky, nor sheepish, nor defiant, nor distant. He wanted to know exactly how his father died and he asked how his mother was taking it; he asked about certain relatives and whether his two Turkish uncles had come forward to help with the funeral arrangements. He said he wished his mother could come to Oxford but Nuri bey pointed out that it would be impossible, at least for a few weeks. Then Jason said he would very much like to be able to go home but at the moment his commitments did not permit of it. Nuri bey said that his mother understood completely that, with his final examinations coming along, it would be impossible. Jason said there were things more important than his Finals and Nuri bey exclaimed "Surely not!" Lady Mercia had told Jason that Nuri bey knew everything; Jason did no explaining, he said quite frankly and openly that he was looking after a young girl who was more important than any Finals. "I hope to marry her," he said, "but unfortunately I cannot do so until I am twenty-one without written permission from parent or guardian."

"You should have no difficulty in getting permission from your mother," Nuri bey said smoothly. "But you are only twenty at present, is it not rather young?"

"Unfortunately, at the moment there is a summons out for her arrest for breach of probation order. She got very wild one night and knocked off a policeman's helmet; since then they've been trying to find her and if they do . . . if they do, she will be sent to one of those awful places, a detention centre with a lot of delinquent kids probably for three months."

"I see," Nuri bey said with infinite restraint.

"And I have to stay hidden, too; I don't want to be murdered by that frightful creature Arnika, a so-called friend of my father. He actually came here on Thursday; I'm afraid he followed you here and then came alone the next day to see what he could find out for himself. Fortunately Aunt Mercia was able to deal with him and he hasn't a clue that I'm here. I'm glad to have the gun, thanks!"

Jason got up and walked up and down the room, fingers tucked into the top of his jeans. "He's a fanatic, that man. He's not human at all. He's predatory, like an animal who only lives to hunt, but even an animal stops now and then to *eat* his prey. This beast doesn't; he spends his whole life plotting, scheming to make money out of growing and selling raw opium but when he's made it, he never sits down anywhere to enjoy it, he's off on the next deal; I've never known if he has a wife and children, or if he ever sits down and eats a meal, or goes to bed at night. I'm certain he never sleeps; he often used to visit my father at two or three a.m."

He sat down opposite Nuri bey again. "He's absolutely ruthless; friendship and loyalty mean nothing to him. He put me in the position of being found with a case full of opium though I think my father would have gone mad if he'd known."

"You don't think your father knew, then?"

"I'm certain he didn't; my father was over-proud of me, he boasted about me to his friends; the money he made out of dope-peddling went, partly, to pay for me at University. He probably mentioned to Arnika I was going back to England and Arnika used me as someone whom the suitcase could go with. You see, you can't send a suitcase off by air alone, it's got to have, *apparently*, someone with it. If *Arnika* had been found shot dead, I should have understood it; my father would have killed him if he had known what he did. You see . . . I'm sure my father never really gave his opium-growing a serious thought; he never once asked himself what was going to happen to it finally, whom it was going to destroy. His mind didn't work like that. I'm sorry for him, in a way."

"If you had left the case where it was . . .?"

"It had a label with my name on it. I suppose you think I might have torn it off and left it where it was? Well, I might, but there would have been a lot more dope going around." He stooped and patted Fido, who was squatting between his feet. "I'm against this drug thing and this was a good chance of doing that damned Arnika out of a good lot of it. I was so angry at the time, unfortunately I didn't realise how awkward it was going to be for me. He's out to get it back at all costs; I'm sure he shot my father and I'm absolutely certain he means to shoot me. He thinks he can carry on his business a lot better without a Yenish as a partner. As soon as I caught sight of him in Oxford, I realised I'd have to disappear for a week or two. I went to a phone box to ring Aunt up to ask if she'd hide me and as I was talking to her, he was standing watching me across the street. I managed to evade him by taking a short cut he doesn't know anything about, running like a stag and getting over the wall of St. John's. Unfortunately I found Ronda in the street, she was actually holding on to a tree in Manor Road; she couldn't stand up. I got a taxi and took her back to her digs and then came here. I brought as many books with me as I could get hold of and I'm working, I promise you I am. I left my luggage at my new lodgings, I knew Arnika would be waiting for me outside, I haven't dared to go back there yet. After I'd been here a few days I had a talk with Aunt Mercia about Ronda and she said we could have the gardener's cottage, out there behind the stable yard. The old man died last year and it had been standing empty. She was trying to get someone else, advertising the job with furnished cottage but everyone wanted it unfurnished and Aunt Mercia was wondering about selling the furniture. She's given up the idea for now and I do as much gardening as I have time for by way of repaying her kindness."

"You oiled the lawn mower and got it going for her."

He nodded, smiling slightly. "And of course, when I heard the gun I thought, no, I *knew*, Arnika had arrived and had killed Aunt Mercia because she wouldn't say where I was. Thank goodness it didn't happen, and thank you, again, for the gun. It will come in useful, as they say." He picked up Fido. "Really a lap dog but what a magnificent house dog! I heard all about the scramble in the shrubbery with Fido in the lead and you shaking Arnika like a doormat; I wish I could have seen it. Aunt Mercia was entranced!"

He played with the dog.

"I should like to meet Miss Ronda," Nuri bey said formally.

"I told her you would probably want to. Aunt Mercia is staying out of the way, dear old thing. Come on."

The cottage was recently built, a workman's dwelling with its newness not yet worn off, the roses that had been lovingly trained up the walls were not yet in leaf. She sat in the living-room beside the gas fire, rocking herself to and fro in an old rocking chair and humming tunelessly; she was wearing black slacks and a black jersey with a polo neck, black socks and a pair of dirty white flat-heeled slippers. She peered out at him, a tiny face from a mass of brown unclean-looking hair, pale, freckled and pointed: she looked not more than thirteen years old.

"Hallo, there!"

Nuri bey held out his hand and after a moment's hesitation she put out her own, giggling slightly. "How do you do," Nuri bey said gravely. In front of the window a trestle table held a number of books, typewriter and manuscript. She saw him looking at them and said: "You see, he is being a good boy and studying . . . sometimes!" She intended Nuri bey to make a remark such as: but he has to study a lot, rather more than sometimes; but he carefully said nothing. He raked about in his mind for a single remark to make that would not sound heavy and out of context. He felt in his pocket for the jewel Tamara had given him; it was safely there. He decided that it was a waste of time trying to make conversation before coming to the point at issue so he plunged right in with his suggestion before allowing a decent time to elapse.

"I hear you haven't been well, my dear," he said kindly. "It would do you good to have a bit of a holiday. Why not come back to Turkey with me and stay for a while with Jason's mother?"

There was a long silence; Jason, sitting sideways in an upright chair, swivelled round slightly to see her better.

"You would like her," Nuri bey said.

No answer.

"She is a most kind and sweet lady, as I am sure Jason has told you. If you could stay in Istanbul, at their lovely house on the Sea of Marmara, you would like it, I am sure. From a bedroom window you can almost throw a stone into the sea and it is so warm and sunny . . ." He tailed off, feeling he was getting nowhere.

She gave a harsh laugh, a really unpleasant sound. "You think I'd be better out of the way whilst Jason gets on wiv his work?"

"On the whole, yes," Nuri bey replied temperately. "Another three months," he spread his hands expressively, "it is nothing."

"What do you think, Jay?" She looked sharply at him through her hair. "Eh? What do you think?"

"He's got something," Jason answered cautiously.

"Oh, you think so, do you?" She laughed again really unpleasantly. "Well, you've got to have a passport for foreign travel, or at least, so I've always heard." She seemed amused and giggled again, tucking her chin down into her high-necked sweater.

"You've got a passport, Ronda."

"You're forgetting, Jasey love, you silly boy. When I was having my second kid," she said to Nuri bey, "I was so browned off I went off to Israel. Some of the boys clubbed together and got me ninety pounds for me. I'd heard about these *Kibbutz*, they're camps where you all live for the community. I thought it'd be just the job." She giggled again. "So off I went, very preggy, mind. Living for the community, eh? There was nothing like that; they took one look at me, one look, mind, and shut the door in my face. I went round, all over the place; the same thing happened four times. I hadn't a penny left, I had to come back and they sent me by air in one of their jets for free. At least, it wasn't for free, they said they was lending me the fare and they kept my passport as a guarantee, they called it. When I got the money I could send them the fare, and they'd return it, so they said. Eh, dear me!" she sighed.

Nuri bey did not feel kind any longer; he turned away, looking out of the window, to hide the expression of anger on his face.

"So you see," Jason put in quietly, "just how destitute she is."

"There's your Aunt Maisie," Nuri bey said, still not turning round. "A very kind person, and very worried about you."

Ronda's giggle turned to a shriek of laughter. "I can't go there."

"Why not?"

"There's Stan," she went on laughing hideously. "Her husband, she wouldn't have a happy moment with me in the house . . ." She said something else so disgusting that Nuri bey could barely believe that he had heard it.

Jason looked pained; he got up and touched Nuri bey's arm. "You don't understand," he said in Turkish.

"It isn't a question of understanding," Nuri bey cried angrily. "Jason, Jason! Marshallah! Where are your senses? This thing you're doing is not clever, it is not kind, it is not compassionate; you cause far more unhappiness with your actions than you do happiness." Nuri bey put his hands on Jason's shoulders and searched the good-looking young face. "Have pity on yourself, man, do not behave like an adolescent schoolboy, nurturing a rattlesnake which will surely grow up and kill you." But he realised that words were useless. Jason's face now bore an expression at once resentful and stubborn.

"Now you are looking just like your father!" Jason wrenched himself away.

Whilst they talked Ronda was muttering to herself: "Listen to the wind!" She shivered and reached for a dishcloth-coloured knitted garment which she struggled into and wrapped round herself: "Ugh! The beastly moaning wind!" A sharp March breeze was whining through the group of pines which grew in front of the cottage. "The nasty moaning wind, how I hate it!" She rocked herself more energetically and groaned out a negro spiritual with the constant refrain: *Ah'm comin' Lord, Ah'm comin' very soon.* Her eyes had a strange unfocused look.

"You don't understand," Jason repeated, "she has nobody in the world who cares whether she lives or dies."

"Nonsense," Nuri bey argued, "there is a nice woman probation officer who is genuinely fond of Ronda. She is experienced in dealing with girls like this."

"Please, Nuri bey, that is a foolish remark; the girl needs someone of her own."

Nuri bey shook his head: "Jason, Jason, you are a sentimentalist, can you not see that she is one of the world's unfortunates? She wishes to lead the kind of life she has lived. As I see her, rocking away there, she is filled with rebellion. . . ."

"I know you're talking about me," Ronda said slyly.

". . . as I see it, dear boy, she is your prisoner."

"No, no! Nuri bey, you are wrong. She is like the woman buried at Eyup upon whose gravestone are carved the words: '*I have come into the garden of this world but have found no kindness.*' You and I are Turks, Nuri bey, and our great modern prophet Atatürk decreed that we are not an Eastern but a Western state." He went on in Turkish: "But no amount of thinking will ever make us European; we're Eastern entirely and in the marrow of our bones we believe that a woman has no soul."

"And so you wish to disprove this, Jason my dear? Alas, you could not have chosen a worse specimen upon which to try out your theories. If you had wished to experiment with Hannah, now . . ."

"Hannah?"

"Miss Hannah Benson."

Ronda was looking at him through her hair and Nuri bey looked boldly back at her.

"Hannah?" Jason repeated, as though this were some strange new thought which had just occurred to him.

"What a lovely girl . . ." Nuri bey had been about to say things like *clean* and *pure* and *beautiful* but he was beginning to learn that these words would have no immediate appeal. "A lovely *healthy* girl," he said, "not a sickly weakling but a woman worthy of any man. This, this situation is degrading to anyone calling himself a man: it is the work of an emotional woman that you are doing, a nurse, dedicated to her job, would be as devoted as you are now. This is not love nor kindness nor compassion but . . ." he paused for words—"an agitation of mind . . ."

"Take no notice of him, Jasey," Ronda advised, "it sounds very nasty. Miss Hannah Benson, he said! It don't sound as though he's on our side, Jasey. Send him away. God, it's boring enough here; it's a pity our first visitor has come to preach!"

Nuri bey turned his back on her and returning to the window, he brought out the little washleather bag and, calling Jason to him, still with his back to the room, held the pearl, amethyst and diamond cross in the palm of his hand.

"Your mother gave me this to sell for you. I do not like to do this important thing alone; will you come to London with me?"

Jason turned the ornament over and examined it carefully. "What a beautiful thing; it is a pity to sell it."

"If it is a matter of keeping this girl for years—"

"For years?"

"That is what you evidently intend to do. You will need money for it and as your mother is now a widow there will not be any allowance available."

"Ah'm comin', Lord
Ah'm comin' very soon."

Nuri bey slipped the cross back into the bag. "Tomorrow morning on the nine o'clock train? I have looked up the time and I have also the address of the gem-merchant in the City of London." He patted his pocket as though to reassure himself that it was safe and looked round the room. "You are quite comfortable here even though it is not of the quality to which you have been accustomed," Nuri bey said tranquilly, "but you cannot allow Lady Mercia to keep you indefinitely."

"I repay with labour as well as rent."

"So I see from your hands," Nuri bey returned smoothly. "Do you think there is a chance that you will pass your exams?"

"I may have to ask the college for another year."

Nuri bey raised his eyebrows: "You do intend to return to the University?"

Jason looked out of the window, finger tips in the top of his jeans.

"Yes or no?" Nuri bey persisted.

"Oh, come on, you two!" Ronda moaned.

"It has been known that they give another year."

"But on what ground? That you have been otherwise engaged, living with a drug-taking whore?"

"Oh, be quiet, damn you!" Jason shouted. He stamped about the room.

"Take no notice of him, Jasey."

"Forgive me, Jason, I am in the position of your parents at the moment. No one has told you what a fool you are; it is my unfortunate duty to have to do so."

"Well, that's not the way to do it . . .!"

Ronda was looking from one to the other, not understanding a word but getting the general gist. "That's right, Jason, the interfering old square," she said encouragingly but only succeeding in making Jason wince. There was a long pause before Nuri bey said quietly: "There is now no problem because I myself will dispose of Arnika and you will be at liberty to leave here and return to college. And as for Ronda, sooner or later they will find her; someone will tell the police that she is here. So, you see, there is no longer any problem, dear boy."

"What nonsense! You can't turn into a murderer!"

Ronda made a gruesome face, then put out a long, thin tongue.

"Can't I? You will see," Nuri bey said grimly. "I have only to be careful; I shall need to think when and where. At present I feel it will not be in Oxford but in London where we have the River Thames . . ."

"The Thames isn't the Bosphorus, you know."

"I am well aware that the Thames is not the Bosphorus, it is neither so deep nor so wide nor so swift-running. The Bosphorus is not a river. But I think the Thames will do. It will be one or the other."

Lady Mercia was pruning the roses in the sunken garden at the opposite side of the house. "This is my favourite job," she said. "Look at the lovely pruning scissors dear Miranda gave me for my last birthday. Pick up the pieces and put them in the barrow for me, dear Nuri bey. Tell me, how did you get on?"

"Not well, not at all well."

"It is a problem, is it not?"

"A very big problem. I think, with luck, Jason will be coming to London with me to-morrow. Ronda will be spending the day by herself."

"Yes?"

"May I advise you not to see anything that may happen."

She stopped working and looked at him. "You're not going to do anything silly?"

"What do you mean by silly?"

"Tell the probation people where she is?"

"Why not?"

"Because Jason needs curing of her *more than* relieving of her."

Nuri bey was filled with admiration but he merely said: "I have a better idea but it may not come off. If it does not, in desperation I may have to tell Miss Smith."

"Don't do it; there's no cure that way. I could have told the probation people myself long ago if I had thought it would do any good."

"I am going now," Nuri bey said, "but before I go I must tell you that I have thought over what you said about there being one thing greater than the longing for drugs, and that is the longing for affection. Well, you may be right in some cases but I don't think you are in this one. You said you were not a sentimentalist but I think you are. You believe that Jason is doing some good, don't you? I don't. All Jason is doing is ruining his life."

She went on pruning steadily and Nuri bey continued to pick up the pieces of rose stem as she let them drop; they hurt him and pierced his fingers but he did not notice.

"I do not know English well enough to make my point excellently but I believe the girl is entirely physical with nothing whatever in her mind and I believe she can only be, as it were, spoken to on those terms."

"Merely a man's point of view," she returned stubbornly.

"Lady Mercia," Nuri bey bowed slightly, wiping his fingers with his handkerchief, "I go now to catch the bus. Please do not appear to-morrow . . ."

"I shall continue to prune the roses," she said firmly, "and, as you can see, I am not within sight or earshot of the cottage. Neither screams nor gunshots will budge me; that is, of course," she looked up at the sky, "if the weather stays nice."

As he walked down the drive, Nuri bey again applied his handkerchief; he found his fingers were bleeding slightly in several places.

10

Dear Miss Hannah Benson,
Will you very kindly come at once to my hotel; I wish to speak with you about a certain person for whom we have both much regard.

Yours,
Hurry please. *Nuri Iskirlak*
(Nuri bey)

As he returned to his hotel, Nuri bey had seen him, sitting in the coffee bar next door; he looked away instantly but he knew that he had been seen.

He sent the chef's schoolboy son with the note, who soon returned, saying that he had put it in the young lady's hand. Nuri bey stood waiting for her at the door of the hotel and when he saw her bicycling down St Giles' towards him he stepped forward smiling.

He took her into the coffee bar next door to his hotel and, ignoring Arnika who, he could see in a mirror which covered one wall, was glowering savagely, took a seat as far away from him as possible. He watched him take out his dark glasses and put them on and he saw him order another cup of coffee as he talked to Hannah.

"I have found Jason but it is no matter for rejoicing; he is living in a small cottage near here with the girl Ronda and it is as you guessed, he thinks he is curing her and he wishes to marry her." To fill in the vibrating pause he said: "He is a pursuer of lofty but impracticable ideals." He looked affectionately at her, now so like Jenny with her baby pouting mouth but also a young woman with something in her head. She said, quite unpleasantly: "A tiny, new-style Don Quixote."

Nuri bey hastened to defend him, saying that she must remember that he was an extraordinary mixture of races, he could not be labelled haphazardly. He was still very young.

"The same age as me."

"But two years behind in development."

She took no notice of that but glared down into her coffee cup.

"Have some sugar," Nuri bey suggested and, after she had drunk a little coffee, he said that Jason must be cured, to which Hannah snapped back, with all the wisdom of her years, that you could not cure people, they were what they were. Jason was a write-off.

Not at all, not at all, Nuri bey argued. Jason's father had been mixed up with people in Istanbul who made money from growing and exporting the raw material of drugs for the illicit sale to drug-takers. He had found himself at London Airport with a suitcase full of the stuff attached to himself; rather than let it go back into the hands of the people who intended to sell it in England, he kept it, and brought it to Oxford with him. Since then he had been in hiding from the people who were determined to get the valuable consignment back, so much so that they had murdered his father. Jason was, in fact, made out to be something of a hero.

Nuri bey could not see her face for the hair that hung down between them.

"Are you sure they murdered his father?"

"He was found shot dead in his library. I am sure they believed that his father had instructed Jason to sell the consignment privately so that he could keep the money for himself and that amounted to quite a lot of money . . ."

She was staring down into her empty coffee cup and Nuri bey ordered more.

"So what do you say, Hannah?"

"What do you want me to do?"

"I am not quite sure; I am only a man and a foreigner; I can only grope about in my mind as to what to do with Ronda. But to-morrow I am taking Jason away to London for the day, at least, I hope I am. He is going to need a lot more money and, with his father dead, he doesn't know where he is going to get it. I have some," he patted his pocket, "from his mother, but he will have to come to London with me if he wishes to have it."

"I see," she said thoughtfully. "So she's going to be alone to-morrow and you think I can take the probation people to her?"

"Not quite as simple as that. Don't you see? If Jason comes home and finds her gone it is not going to *cure* him, the first thing he will do is to rush frantically to her aid. If she is sent to a detention centre, he will be visiting her there whenever possible with comforts of every kind . . ."

"Don't make me sick."

"But that's the way it is! And I'll tell you this: she's lonely there in the cottage with him, she misses the excitement of the life she's led in Oxford. She is bored to death, she's had two months of it now and she hates it up there. She never sees anyone but Jason and he won't allow her to have any more dope than he thinks radically necessary. I *reely* believe she would get away if she had the slightest chance."

"How could she? She has nowhere else to go! Wishful thinking, Nuri bey."

He sat back with arms folded, lips set in a firm line. "Then *you* think, Hannah. You love the boy, *you* think of something."

He paid for the coffee and they went out into St. Giles.

"All my life I have longed to see this city," Nuri bey said pathetically, "now I am here and I have lost all taste for that which I wished to see."

"And what was that?"

"Partly the beautiful old city itself and partly the wonderful books and manuscripts, the illuminated, priceless old books in the Bodleian, the Sarum Ordinal printed by Caxton in 1477 of which there is only one known copy, the first illuminated book ever printed in the City of London, that is the Book of Hours on vellum with woodcuts, the Sarum Missal . . ."

"Poor Nuri bey!" She took his arm and guided him across the road. "Let me, at least, show you what they have done to St. John's College."

The sun had come out from behind a cloud and shone on the newly cleaned, wet stone so that he felt uplifted and lyrical.

"Do you think she has sex with him?"

He jumped but pulled himself together enough to say calmly:

"No, no, I do not. Or is that wishful thinking?"

But she was too absorbed in her own thoughts to smile at his slight joke. "I bet you're wrong. What a nuisance sex is!"

"But *reely*, I don't. She is a sick, miserable, little cat."

"You don't know," Hannah murmured darkly. "Sex is at the bottom of everything:

Amoebas at the start
Were not complex
They tore themselves apart
And started sex."

Nuri bey pursed his lips to suppress the smile. "Where did you get that?"

"I don't know. I'm reading English; I read so much, it must have come from somewhere because it's always popping into my mind."

They had strolled out of the quads and across the garden. They were still arm-in-arm, much to Nuri bey's delight and, as they turned round to retrace their steps, he nudged her: "See?"

Beautifully intelligent, she saw at once: "Your square man with a walk like a swan on land. He's still following you!"

"Not always, but nearly always. When I take a great deal of trouble to shake him off, he doesn't; as for instance to-day when I went to see Jason in his hideout. But he was waiting in the coffee bar for me to come back. He'll wait and wait and wait, he never tires."

"Yes, I saw him watching us."

"I enjoyed it yesterday . . . When I went to see the football match, I left him standing in a long queue; my friends and I already had seats! I don't know whether he got in or not."

Arnika was now strolling ahead of them, doubtless hoping that he would be taken for any sightseer. Outside Nuri bey's hotel she took up her bicycle from where she had left it leaning against the wall.

"I haven't thought of anything yet but will you give me her address?"

"She is living in the gardener's cottage at Coverley Court, by kind permission of Jason's great aunt, Lady Mercia Mossop. But if you go, go straight past the house and through the stable yard; Lady Mercia prefers to be left out of this affair."

She listened carefully. "The man who is following you has walked right down to the Martyrs' Memorial," she said, "but he can still see us perfectly clearly. How can you stand it, Nuri bey?"

"I cannot," he returned cheerfully, "and very soon I shall have to do something about it."

He risked Arnika seeing him with Jason but it was a risk which he was prepared to take because even Jason would realise that this expedition should be undertaken because he could not do much without money. He rose early and breakfasted in a hurry, asking permission from the chef to leave by the back entrance in order to get to the station more quickly. He went into the refreshment room on the opposite side of the main line to the London platform and watched the barrier for an hour for Arnika's relentless appearance. Three minutes before the London train came in, he went over to the London platform and as the train came in he saw Jason buying a ticket and greeted him casually as he came through the barrier. The train drew out and there was no sign of Arnika.

Jason was not prepared to talk; he had brought a book with him and he sat in the crowded second-class carriage opposite Nuri bey and his head was bent over his book during the whole hour-long journey. They took a bus to the City of London, where Nuri bey looked around him with great interest and pleasure, and eventually found the gem-merchant in a big block of offices overlooking St. Paul's. He seemed a friendly and honest man; he told them that none of the pieces he had sold in the past for Tamara's mother had been so elaborate, so grand or so beautiful as the cross they had brought now. He, personally, did not feel he could offer them the sum it was undoubtedly worth. He suggested they would probably get more than it was worth if they took it to an auctioneer in Bond Street who held regular jewel sales at which one could obtain the best prices in the world.

Nuri bey insisted on seeing round St. Paul's Cathedral, he also wanted to walk along the Embankment as far as the Houses of Parliament, see Big Ben and Westminster Abbey. After that they were tired and Nuri bey generously offered luncheon at the Hilton Hotel. It was after half past three when they came out into Park Lane, well lined with excellent food and drink, and walked slowly in the early spring sunshine to Bond Street.

The auctioneers accepted the gem with well-concealed pleasure, as being a genuine Russian heirloom, and locked it away in their safe until the next jewel sale. They would give no definite figure but suggested a reserve price of four figures.

Out in Bond Street again, almost reeling with the delight of success, Nuri bey declared that he must go to the British Museum; it would have been churlish of Jason not to come too. They stayed three hours and, returning to Paddington, they caught a train with a dining car back to Oxford.

Over dinner Jason relented; he dropped the formal manner in which he had behaved all day; he suggested that he buy a bottle of wine, then said he had enjoyed his day.

"And you haven't been followed," he murmured, smiling slightly, "have you?"

"No," Nuri bey returned, holding his glass towards Jason in a toast. "I drink to to-day, one of the most delightful I have ever spent. To-day each of us has been free as air, we have both shed our *incubi*!" *Incubus* meaning evil spirit, Jason might have taken the remark badly but he didn't, he went on smiling as he sipped his wine and Nuri bey thought there might still be hope.

They parted at the station, Jason to take a taxi back to Coverley and Nuri bey to walk swiftly through the streets to his hotel. He deliberately went by the Randolph and noticed, as he passed, a poster propped against a newspaper stand saying:

LABOURERS' DWELLING EXPLOSION

OXFORD WOMAN KILLED

He strode across Beaumont Street hoping that Arnika would be idly watching through a window of the hotel and would futilely end what must have been an entirely fruitless day, in following him the remaining hundred yards to his hotel. Whether he did or not, he did not know because when he got to his hotel he felt so tired by the tension and by the concentrated sightseeing that he went straight to bed and slept heavily until morning.

Whilst he was having breakfast, Maisie arrived upon the scene, flustered, untidy and inclined to weep. Where had he been all yesterday? In London with Jason, he said happily. She asked breathlessly if he could prove it and he had said certainly he could, several times over. But why? Was he sure, she pressed him, that Jason was with him? But certainly, it could be proved by many people; they had paid several visits, had lunched at an hotel, had been to the British Museum for several hours.

Maisie looked nervously round the dining-room. Was there somewhere they could talk? Nuri bey took her up to the unused small lounge on the first floor. "Now, tell me," he said calmly. "What is wrong?"

Maisie burst into noisy sobs, then mopping up her face she told him. Yesterday morning, about twelve-thirty, the gardener's cottage at Coverley Court had "been blown sky-high" and Ronda's body had been found in the wreckage. Nuri bey said nothing, his mouth remained a grim thin line but there was a great light in his eyes.

"On the surface," Maisie said, "it looks like suicide but no one believes that, least of all me. She wouldn't do a thing like that, not Ronda. But someone did it, gas taps don't turn themselves on."

"Gas taps?"

"Remember? They had gas in every room, same as they have at the big house; there wasn't no electricity because it was too expensive to bring underground; the old ladies wouldn't have it overhead like everybody else because they said it would spoil the view!" she shrieked. She was slightly hysterical; she said the police had been round to her place within an hour, seeing that Lady Mossop had told them whose the body was. She'd been questioned left, right and centre and her husband had been called home from work and they had both gone to identify the body in the mortuary. At which she burst into renewed sobs.

Without appearing to hurry her home, Nuri bey managed to put her into a taxi and took her back to her house, telling her to take an aspirin and go to bed. He left her moaning as to what the neighbours must have thought yesterday when there were no less than two police cars outside the house.

He himself took the taxi on to Coverley where he found Lady Mercia and Fido sitting by the fire, Lady Mercia finishing her breakfast from a tray across her knees. She was pale and slightly distraught but perfectly ready to discuss the events.

"Dear Nuri bey, I must be a wicked old woman but nothing seems to me to matter but that our problem is solved. You told me to take no notice of anything that might happen through the stable yard, was it this you had in mind?"

He leaned across, saying earnestly: "I swear that it was not."

Then what had he in mind when he had told her to keep out of the way? He retaliated by reminding her that she had said that neither screams nor gunshots would send her out; what had *she* had in mind?

"I felt that anything could occur after what has already happened with you fighting in the shrubbery and firing guns into the air; it was a perfectly natural remark under the circumstances."

They stared at one another.

"What did happen?" Nuri bey almost croaked.

"I don't know," she croaked back.

"What do you *think* happened?"

"I do not permit myself the luxury of *thinking*."

"Then tell me the facts."

"I can only tell you what I know. When I was preparing my luncheon in the kitchen there was a very loud explosion, the windows rattled and a pan which had been on the edge of a shelf, fell off with a noise which frightened me more than the explosion. I thought it was the much-talked-of atom bomb, gone off at last! In spite of your warnings I went out: there was a cloud of dust rising behind the stable yard. I hurried through the yard and saw the cottage on fire. I ran back and dialled for the fire engine; it took twenty minutes to come."

She paused and looked at Nuri bey very directly. "In the meantime," she said clearly, "I let it burn. I sat in here with Fido and let it burn. You couldn't expect an old lady of eighty-two to start fire-fighting, could you? I have only a few fire extinguishers and they are too heavy for me to carry."

Nuri bey could have smiled but he was careful not to do so.

"As soon as the firemen came, they very bravely turned off the gas at the cottage main and had the fire out in a few minutes. They took away the body and I went to see the damage. The cottage is wrecked. I'm only worried about the insurance; the man is coming this morning but what am I going to say to him? Was it Act of God? Of course it wasn't! Every gas tap in the cottage was turned on, that is, the gas fires in the two bedrooms, the living room, the gas oven, the gas burners on top of the stove, everything."

"But how did the explosion happen?"

"By the one small burner left alight in the geyser in the downstairs bathroom, which leads off the kitchen. That's always left on so that when you turn on the bathroom taps, it lights the burners automatically. The bathroom door must have been left ajar. But gas was pouring into the living room all morning and, in the opinion of the police doctor, Ronda was dead long before the explosion. She was sitting in the rocking chair in the living-room when they found her and they are doing a post mortem now. From her colour when they found her they say they are almost sure they will find her lungs full of gas. The explosion blew the bathroom to smithereens and the fire it caused raged through the cottage but very rapidly so that the body wasn't burned badly. They say the colour of her face was unmistakably that of carbon monoxide poisoning. Two unsmoked marihuana cigarettes near a box of matches were found amongst the rubble of the living-room ceiling, which fell all over everything. One might think that Ronda started to light one, but with the concentration of gas that there must have been to cause the explosion, she would have already been unconscious, so they seem to think.

"Well, I had a good talk to Jason last night; he tells me he carefully hid the bottle of 'heroin jam' before he left. He thinks she looked for it as soon as he left but she couldn't have found it, it was buried somewhere in the grounds; he wasn't taking any risks! He had a bottle of whisky, half full in the kitchen cupboard but as everything is wrecked in the kitchen, we can't say whether, in desperation, she drank that or not. They had an old-fashioned gramophone, the sort that you wind by hand, and it seemed she had that on; there were broken records lying about. He says that when he has left her before, she amused herself playing old records and reading her romances; he wasn't worried about her yesterday, more than usual."

There was an insistent ringing of a bell. "That's the back door." Lady Mercia hurried from the room, leaving Nuri bey thoughtfully staring into the fire. She returned almost at once with the milkman who, delivering milk at the cottage, had been horrified at what he had found and had hurried back to the big house to ask what had happened. Only yesterday morning, he said, he had taken the milk to the cottage as usual and the young person had come to the door asking him if he would take her down to the road in his van so that she could hitch a lift into Oxford. He knew she hadn't been well but said that, if she wanted to go all that much, she could walk. She said that the old woman (he apologised to Lady Mercia) was always on the look-out, the young man she lived with would have told his aunt to keep a careful watch on her whilst he was away. The milkman had said he didn't want to get mixed up in anything and furthermore he was busy: good-morning! At which, he told them even more apologetically, she started shouting at him; she ran across the yard whilst he reversed his van and tried to box his ears through the window; he drove off and that was about it.

Nuri bey asked what time that would have been and he replied that he came the same time every day, about ten-twenty, like now, he nodded towards the clock. Lady Mercia said that the police would probably call to take a statement from him and saw him away still distinctly upset.

"I suppose that evidence will be very valuable," she murmured.

"Where is Jason?"

She smiled: "He has gone back to his lodgings. He was interviewed by the police as soon as he returned last night; in fact, they took him back to his lodgings. Both you and he are completely in the clear."

"But of course," he murmured.

"But look here, my dear man, there is no *of course* about it. Jason could have left the gas taps on. You could have doubled back from your postponed journey and turned them on. This was not an Act of God in the way the insurance company mean, but it certainly was in every other way." She sat down heavily. "One thing is quite certain, whenever you *want* someone to die they never do, not that I have ever wanted anybody to die but in the case of poor little Ronda it was so obviously the best thing for her to do; she never should have been born."

Nuri bey said slowly: "There is no doubt that Jason and I were in London yesterday; we went on the nine o'clock and returned on the seven-fifteen from Paddington and at every point during our day they can 'check up on us,' as you call it."

"Then," Lady Mercia returned, pinning him almost against the wall with her piercing blue eyes, "then the only possible conclusion we can come to is that she turned on the gas herself in a frenzy of frustration."

"Yes . . . yes . . . yes," Nuri bey stamped as he emphasised it, "that is certainly what she did."

He went to the ladies' college and found Hannah sitting soberly at a big table in her room, working. "I thought you'd come," she said, pushing a chair forward with her foot. "Would you like a milk drink?"

Nuri bey gave her a long, enquiring look. "Have you seen Jason?"

"No, but I have read last night's *Oxford Mail*; I know what has happened to Ronda, if that is what you mean. It's the talk of the town."

"It is?"

"Well, of course . . ."

"For the love of Allah," Nuri bey said tetchily, "tell me what happened yesterday?"

"Happened?" She sat down and looked at him exceptionally candidly. "Well, Nuri bey, you asked me to do what I could, so directly I had finished breakfast I took my bicycle down to the bus stop, left it there in the car park and got a bus to Coverley village."

"What time?"

"The ten o'clock bus, they go every two hours, and you said Jason would probably be going with you on the nine o'clock train. The bus goes on much farther so I don't think anyone noticed me particularly. I walked up the drive; what a long one it is!"

"Did you see anyone?"

"Not a soul."

"Not the milkman driving away?"

"I saw nobody and nobody saw me, as far as I know. I found the cottage okay and banged on the door. She came to the door in a frightful temper, I could see it the moment I looked at her face. She was wearing her black jersey and slacks and a dreadful scowl and she asked what the hell I wanted . . . very rude. I pushed my way in, I wasn't going to be kept standing out on the doorstep. I sat down when I got inside and said this that and the other."

"What was that?"

"Does it matter? Besides, I can't remember everything I said." There was a long pause and then she admitted: "Oh, well; we had a bit of a scrap in the end."

"A scrap?"

"A . . . a sort of fight; I shook her and she . . ." Hannah pushed up the sleeve of her jersey and showed a strange mark on her forearm. "Where she bit me and here . . ." she demonstrated several scratches on her neck which might have been done by a cat: "she scratched!" She pulled down her sleeve and said: "You would call it very unladylike."

"Not at all, our ladies often bite and scratch."

"Well, ours don't! Then she threw herself down on the sofa and screamed hysterically; she wanted her dope, her heroin jam she called it, and Jason had cleverly hidden it, so she was out of control."

"Then you said good-bye?"

"I didn't bother to say good-bye, she was beyond taking it in. I just went."

"How long were you there?"

"Not quite sure, not more than half an hour, just about that I should guess."

"Then you walked down the drive and caught a bus back."

"Um, except that it wasn't a bus, someone stopped and gave me a lift back to Oxford."

"Then what do you think of it, Hannah? Do you think that when you left she turned on all the gas taps in the house?"

"Must have."

"Was she in a fit state to do so?"

"She was in a state to do anything. How do you suppose the explosion happened?"

"They say the bathroom geyser had a small permanent flame which caused it because the bathroom door must have been left open."

"I see." She fiddled with her pencils and rubbers.

"Does any person know you went to Coverley yesterday morning?"

Keeping her eyes lowered she said: "I haven't told anyone."

"Then don't, there is no point in doing so. You would have to give evidence at the inquest and why should you advertise it that you knew the girl?"

"Um."

After a very long pause indeed Nuri bey said: "This morning Jason is back in his lodgings and, I take it, at work too. He'll have to do his own explaining to the authorities! There seems nothing more for me to do, I may now return to my country and report to his mother that all is as well as we could expect."

"There is something else I did . . ."

"Something *else* . . .?"

"You asked me to help you and I have only done what I could. As I rode back from the bus stop, passing your hotel I saw your old follower, the Turk, sitting as usual in the coffee bar. I went in and told him that both you and Jason had gone back to Istanbul; I said you had both left by the nine o'clock train and would be flying yesterday."

"Marshallah!"

"Did I not do right?"

"Yes, yes, of course."

"I thought it was about time you shook him off and with Jason now around . . ."

Nuri bey was dumbfounded. "You have done marvellously well," he exclaimed, "but has he believed you?"

"From the look on his face I should say so. Would you not have believed me?"

"Since I am becoming more acute in the study of people, thanks to my friend Landrake, I would say . . . no."

He had jumped up and was now pacing the room. This girl whom he hardly knew had, with calm intelligence, wiped out the need for him to remain in England another hour. He could fly back to Tamara and home to-day.

"Hannah," he said, "you English girls are amazing to me; I should like to get to know you better. I have known only one other English girl and she had some of the qualities you have. Above all, she had the amazing ability that you possess: she used her brain; it is something that we do not understand. You have origination."

"Initiative, you mean."

"The one I knew found herself with a case of raw opium and, without a word to anyone, threw the contents into the Golden Horn. It was worth a great deal of money." He paused and walked another round of the table. "I want you to do the same; the contents of Jason's case should be at the bottom of the Isis!"

"Goodness no, it is much too small a river. Someone will fish it out at the end of his punt pole. If it is as important as all that, I'll take a morning off and go up to Town on a day ticket and chuck it in the Thames."

"Do you mean London? Would you do this, Hannah?"

"Yep. Where is it?"

"I think," Nuri bey said slowly, "indeed I am sure, it is in the garden of Latimer College, buried at the top of a little hill in the centre of the lawn, where there is an old grave . . ."

"Good crummy! Shall I have to take a spade with me?"

"I do not think so for I believe Jason buried it with his hands. You will see where the old black soil at the edge of the broken gravestone has been agitated. I should have found it myself but I was disturbed by the Dean."

"The Dean! Ho ho! I can deal with him. Leave it to me, Nuri bey, I'll get rid of it, I promise you." She pulled out an old zip-fastened canvas bag from under a sofa. "I'll use this. Put down your address for me and I'll write and tell you it's done, just to set your mind at ease."

"There is more I must ask of you, my dear girl, I must go at once and I cannot say farewell to Jason. If I am lucky, I may be able to catch the same plane as Arnika, therefore I cannot stay another hour. Will you say farewell for me, and will you ask him to say the same to his aunt and thank her for all she has done? And finally, dear girl, will you send me the newspaper in which the inquest of Ronda is written?"

"I'll do all that," and as he paused by the door and as she stood in front of him, for one golden moment he thought she might be going to give him a quick kiss, as Jenny had done on one fabulous occasion. But no, she was not quite Jenny. She put out a hand and touched his face: "Go safely," she said, "Godspeed; it's been nice knowing you."

11

He threw everything haphazard into the old carpet bag which he had packed so carefully in Istanbul. He called in at a store and, on the advice of the manager, sent a bottle of excellent sherry to Harp, to Aunt Maisie (who would have preferred port), to Lady Mercia, to Miss Smith and to Jason. He went into Blackwell's and carefully chose a book for Hannah, *The Oxford Companion to English Literature*, which he said on a small card he hoped would be useful, and sent his love.

He paid a last visit to the post office and four hours later he was airborne. He had to take the night plane to Rome, where he had to change, and another to Athens. He had no doubt that Arnika would be in Istanbul by now and sent a wire to Landrake to tell him. It was dusk when the plane took off, the end of a fantastic day, not from the point of view of physical happenings but from the state of his mind.

The longer I live, he mused, the more I find I have to learn and he looked back at the land where the sun goes down, as they used to do in his country in the old days, and marvelled.

But in Rome there was an inexplicable delay of nearly four hours and, when the plane finally arrived at Athens, on its way to Beirut, the Istanbul plane had already left. There was time to spend a night in Athens but Nuri bey's state of mind was such that he decided to sleep in a comfortable chair at the airport. Before breakfast next morning he sent another telegram to Landrake to announce his arrival. When at last his jet touched down at Yesilkoy he looked anxiously amongst the onlookers for Landrake's small distinctive figure. But it was not until he was through the Customs and coming out of the arrival hall that he saw him getting out of his small car and hurrying across.

"Nuri bey, thank goodness you are here!" Landrake looked pale and tired and slightly less than his usual neat self. He tossed the carpet bag into the back of his car and jumped in like a pleased puppy.

"I have much to tell you, dear friend," Nuri bey said happily.

"I'm bursting to hear everything but it must wait for, in the meantime, I have bad news for you which won't wait." He started the car and they drew out of the approach.

"Arnika has probably returned, and you should have received my wire saying so," Nuri bey put in quickly.

"I did, indeed I did, last night. I telephoned to Tamara to tell her but there was no reply. After receiving your wire to say you were on the way, I telephoned again, still no reply. On my way here I called at the house: she has not been back or spent the night there and her car is in the garage."

"Marshallah!" Nuri bey cried in anguish, "Arnika must have gone straight to her; why did I not kill him?"

"I found those two damned maids rushing about like mad things, looking for their mistress. Would you believe it, they were both out last night, at the house of a relative nearby; they go out most evenings; since Yenish died Tamara does not have an evening meal, she sends them out and is alone in that house. I wish, oh, I wish to God she had told me! I would not have allowed it."

Nuri bey held his head in his hands. "Hurry," he urged, "hurry!"

"But hurry *where*?"

"It must be Arnika . . ."

"Then how is it possible since he has *not* returned? My man was alerted to watch more closely than ever."

Landrake drove to the Yenish house; one of the frightened-looking maids let them in and they went upstairs to the big library overlooking the shimmering sea. Nuri bey looked out of the window; not once during his trip abroad had he seen sunshine like this and the thought flashed through his head: perhaps a great deal of sun was bad for a nation, it stifled, what was the word? *initiative.* It was pure inertia which had stopped him from killing Arnika.

"Sit down and let us be calm, Nuri bey. I must first tell you that whilst you have been doing well your end, I, as far as my British Council work has permitted, have been busy this end. I must start right from the beginning, which was two years ago last October when Madame Miasma was drowned and her servant hanged, owing to your actions. Well, my friend, with them went the backbone of the exporting of raw opium and at that time there started a certain something about Torgüt Yenish's attitude towards you which caused me to *think*.

"Have you not noticed in the past two years, a change in his manner to you, Nuri? No, I am sure you haven't and that is why I picked that bone with you in the car on the morning I drove you down here, only two weeks ago. You lack curiosity."

"In the past tense, *lacked*," Nuri bey put in.

"Right, lacked, but it was because I had the idea of suggesting to Torgüt that he send *you* to look for his son that I picked at you the way I did. It was Yenish who first planned the purchase of a small piece of land for cultivating opium, and it was Arnika who has been his faithful partner for about twenty years. They had trouble at first in finding the right type of soil to grow it on but in the end they succeeded; the opium poppy needs sandy soil and exposure to the sun. Covering a great deal of their comings and goings under Yenish's legitimate business of tanning leather, they managed to run their own private affair excellently and Yenish has lived in a much better style than he would have been able to do solely from his business.

"This last trouble started when Miasma and the eunuch died; she was his main exporter, a woman of infinite resources; since her death their export side has been a series of hits or misses. They have done every possible variety of the old suitcase trick and their losses have been heavy; thousands of dollars' worth of the stuff has had to be abandoned, and has been impounded by the Customs & Excise of the countries into which it was being taken. I've been to one or two airline detective departments and I've found out all this after putting two and two together in my own mind. They've plenty to do, these security people, and as yet they haven't been able to put their finger on the relatively small septic spot in Turkey.

"I don't know which of them, Torgüt Yenish or Arnika, thought of the evil idea of getting Jason unknowingly to take this last consignment with him to England but both of them underestimated the lad. When he saw that anonymous case standing beside his luggage at London Airport . . . he kept it, didn't he?"

Nuri bey nodded. "He carried it out of the Customs hall in his hand. He saw Arnika's dark glasses in the crowd and knew at once what was happening."

"I think, possibly, his mother told him something; he may have been actually on the look-out for it. Tamara has talked to me quite a lot but not about the Jason part of it. She knows I know but she won't let me know how much she knows. One thing is genuinely certain, Yenish has been frantic about hearing nothing from Jason. He doted on the boy, not because he is a nice chap but because he is *his son*, the way you Easterns do. The son is a status symbol, rather than a person in his own right, is he not?"

Nuri bey did not agree.

"And now, Nuri, where is Tamara?"

Nuri bey pressed his finger tips together and looked out across to the Princes' Islands, not replying.

"Tell me about Arnika, then, is he a killer?"

"No, not a real killer, if he had been he would have killed me; that is, he doesn't kill for the sake of killing, as you would say. He would kill in desperation and *will* kill but he's not . . ."

"Trigger-happy?"

"No. I would say he is not a person but a figure of acquisition, he lives to acquire."

"I have done my best to find out something about him; I cannot find any trace of wife or family. He is as anonymous but as relentless as the tick on a sheep's back. He lives off others, off the weakness of others."

"My English vocabulary having much improved, I understand you perfectly. He is, as you say, one of the world's parasites, it is the nature of him not to give in."

"Not to drop off."

"Exactly."

"You would say he is not rash, nor excitable, nor unpredictable."

"Nor has he any imagination, or . . . or *initiative*."

"Then surely, surely, in this negative tick we haven't an insoluble problem, Nuri? You and I between us?"

"He at least has had the initiative, perhaps, to kill Tamara in reprisal?"

"Reprisal for what?"

"Killing Yenish."

"You don't honestly believe that, do you?" Landrake jumped up. "Look, Nuri bey . . ."

The books, arranged with their spines inwards, presented, at first glance, the same appearance as when Nuri bey had last been in the library, the idea being to protect the spines from the strong sunlight. But now Landrake walked round the room pointing to a space here and there and in the front of each of the spaces that he pointed out there was no tiny label with the name of the book. Some twenty-three books of various shapes and sizes were missing from the packed shelves.

He then led the way up to the flat roof with its small wooden shed in which Tamara's star-gazing instruments were housed. In the centre of the roof, away from the shed, a metal sheet lay on the roof-covering to protect it and on it the remains of a bonfire, some of which had blown away in little drifts of burnt paper all over the roof-top. Landrake poked at the blackened pile with a stick and there was no doubt at all that it was the remains of books which had been deliberately burned. Both men bent low over the charred fragments and Landrake was able to find an actual piece of title page which showed it to be a treatise in German on the culture of opium and similar narcotics.

"These are the books which they needed at the start; they can't have been used for years, but Tamara thought fit to destroy them; she is doing her best to save her husband's reputation, bless her. Next, I must tell you about the rest of the outfit, firm, eagle's nest, or whatever you like to call it. I have taken my Mini across to the Asia side and driven right up beyond the site, to that no-man's-land where I took you in the *Sylvia*, Nuri. Approaching from the land side, I hid the car and went on foot. I went as a gawping tourist, never been to Turkey before and looking for the Black Sea! I found them all right; they are not eagles, my friend, but an old father, mother and four sons with their wives and numerous children, Armenians, they live an entirely isolated life because way back, there's some kind of criminal record though I couldn't anything like get to the bottom of it. I think the old father may be an escapee from the army, or something of the kind; it's only a guess. Anyway, I turned up all goggle-eyed and 'doing the country-side.' I looked singularly stupid and though they seem half-starved they invited me in to eat with them, like the Turkish peasants do.

"I could see the damned stuff growing, only a few inches above ground at the moment, loosely concealed by a fringe of regular crop, Indian corn and so on. They're a thoroughly wild lot; we stammered along in broken Turkish, I gathered they're poor beyond poor. They kept using the Arab word *rashsh*, to deceive, and the Turkish word which I later discovered to be landlord. They seemed to have a pretty hefty chip on their shoulders and were by way of asking me to help; I pretended I couldn't understand a word, and I very nearly couldn't, but I put two and two together and I think they were complaining bitterly that their overseer had not been near them and they lacked all sorts of things, rice and such everyday things which were evidently brought to them regularly from the town.

"Finally I got one of the sons to take me to the nearest point to the Black Sea; that wild, desolate place at the mouth of that little river. They have a few miserable decrepit boats hidden here and there amongst the rushes, which they use for fishing. One of the big complaints is that they have no fuel for their outboard motor but judging from the condition of the boat in which he took me along the marshes, it's a good thing; it certainly wasn't fit to put out to sea in!

"I made it clear that this wasn't the bathing beach I had been looking for and I think, on the way back, I managed to circumnavigate the whole opium growing area, a very few acres, my dear Nuri; I shall blow the whole plantation up easily, I only do not want to blow the family away with it."

"Explosions, not another!" Nuri bey cried.

"Another? It is the easiest and quickest way. Yesterday I went to the police and told them there were renegade Armenians living out there. Giving them time to get safely away I shall take the *Sylvia* and the large quantity of gelignite I have, enough to make a real mess of their few acres, and that will be the end of opium growing in Turkey for the moment, I hope."

"Where is the gelignite now?"

"Stowed away safely in the *Sylvia*."

They were leaning on the railing which ran round the edge of the roof looking out over the wonderfully peaceful scene.

"Great Allah!" Nuri bey cried, "you English and your explosions!"

"There have to be explosions," Landrake said comfortably, "before you can attain peace, sometimes. I was in the Royal Engineers for a time and we exploded our way around. Have you the keys of the *Sylvia* safely, Nuri bey?"

He produced them from his pocket and Landrake nodded. "You may yet need them." But Nuri bey was now examining the little observatory. He tried the handle of the door; it was locked; the blind was drawn over the sloping glass window in the roof. Landrake followed him and he also turned the knob, rattling it impatiently and pushing against the door.

"Shall we break the window?"

Nuri bey said: "Tamara has some valuable apparatus in here, a six-inch reflecting telescope and that spectroscope that was left her by her old professor at the university, and her celestial globe; no, we can't break the window: there might be a storm and if her instruments were damaged she would never forgive us."

Landrake was looking at him in astonishment. "My dear Nuri, do you honestly believe Tamara is a murderer? You think perhaps she has pulled the body of Arnika in here?"

"Anything may have happened," Nuri bey said tetchily, "but it is more likely that *her* body is in here."

They stared at one another across the locked door.

PART THREE

That was Tamara

1

In the evenings Tamara would climb the ladder on to the roof with the happy anticipation of a keen theatregoer in the exciting moment of silence as the curtain rises. She wore her beautiful Russian sable coat because it was chilly up there and often became very cold as she sat spellbound, at her telescope. First she took her revolver out of her handbag and put it down on the table beside her.

Then she uncovered her instrument, then sat on her stool and swivelled round towards the West to find Venus which is sometimes the Morning and sometimes the Evening star; to-night the planet was shining brightly, a crescent, like a baby half-moon, its tips clearly visible through the telescope. She turned on her reading lamp and looked at her notes from last night; she hoped she would some time find a new planet, like Phobos and Deimos, the two little moons of Mars or, as Galileo did in 1610, she might disclose four new planets of Jupiter. The satellites discovered by Galileo with his tiny primitive telescope were called national names like Io and Ganymede but she would call hers Tamara; it was the same ambition that causes people to write their names on cathedral walls, but hers would endure for ever.

The whole firmament was a rushing bustle of traffic, stars swinging round each other, everything going at varying tilts, different angles, in apparently opposite directions, at different speeds, overtaking each other, dropping behind; though she was working on only a few square inches of the heavens Tamara was tremendously busy, turning from her telescope to her notes and making frantic scribbles before turning back to her instrument.

When there was a knock on the door behind her she jumped so violently that she dropped her pencil, she stooped to pick it up as the door opened outwards and Arnika stood there, square and dark in his black overcoat and black hat, one gloved hand upon the door knob.

"Oh, how you shocked me!" she gasped in Turkish, "but I was half-expecting you." She picked up her revolver from where it lay beside her telescope at the same moment as he brought a revolver out of his pocket.

"Since we are both armed it seems foolish to threaten one another." She laughed slightly. "What do you want, Arnika?"

"You know very well what I want. You have done your best to ruin us and you have almost succeeded. You arranged that Jason should steal that last consignment of opium; where is it?"

"I have no idea."

"Where is Jason?"

"He is safe and well," she said and with a small smile brought out of her bag, with one hand, the telegram she had received from Nuri bey. He merely glanced at it.

"It seems Nuri bey has returned with Jason and I am certain that they have brought the opium back with them; I have made enquiries amongst the half-dozen contacts in England and none of them have received this consignment. Our own people over there have already paid for half of it, don't you understand?"

"How can you be sure of anything? They are all probably lying. Anyway, I have nothing whatever to do with it."

"There *you* are lying. You are a vile woman, you destroyed your husband morally and you finally destroyed his body."

"How can you say I destroyed him morally? At the last he actually allowed his beloved son to act as carrier for your foul drug; he was morally destroyed when he allowed his greed to overrule his love for his son. I am glad he died when he did; his greed would have grown worse with age; at least some small portion of his immortal soul may be saved. And, by the way, I did not kill him."

"You Christians!" Arnika spat. "You killed him to 'save his immortal soul'! That is a good one, I must say."

Tamara wanted to cover her telescope and put her notes together but she did not dare to turn her back. Though shaking inside, she was still starry-eyed when she said: "What a machine you are, you move automatically, you're always on the make and you don't do anything at all that is not directed to that end. You're a kind of computer; how *boring* for you." And in English she added: "You're a small suppurating non-entity and I hate you."

It was lost on him. He argued: "It is business; one has others to consider as well as oneself. Now that Yenish is gone there is only myself as overseer and I have to pay my employees, if I do not they will cease to work for me."

Tamara laughed a little: "Why should I care?"

"Because you, too, will be involved."

"Not at all," she cried, "I knew nothing at all about Torgüt's affairs . . ."

"You lie, you lie, you lie! You sent Nuri Iskirlak to England to find Jason, he succeeded where I failed, and now they tell me he has brought your son home; where are they?" His voice rose to a sudden wave of anger: "Tell me or I shall shoot. No one knows I am here, the house door was unlocked; I shall slip away and no one will know that I have killed you."

"Oh, yes they will. They will know that whoever has shot me also shot Torgüt; you will never be able to go back to your opium plantation because a friend of mine now knows all about it, where it is and who farms it; *he* has reported the whole affair to the police."

She could only see Arnika's face from the light of her reading lamp which was reflected down on to her desk but she could see that he had taken on that gangrenous look. She was sure, then, that he was going to shoot her; there was nothing left for him to do.

She said carefully: "Nuri bey and Jason are not here but Jason has been and gone; he has left a case . . ."

"Ah . . ." Arnika shouted. "Can it be that he has returned with the opium because he could not find a market?"

Tamara bowed her head, looking at the gun in her hand, which was shaking visibly. "If you will put away your gun, I will put away mine, here in my handbag."

Arnika gave her a long sulky look. "Very well." He slipped it back in his overcoat pocket and she calmly covered her telescope, drew the blind, gathered her notes together, turned out the lamp, then shut and locked the door, putting the key and the revolver in her handbag.

"I will go first," she said, hanging her handbag over her arm. "I will fetch the case," she murmured outside the library.

"I will come with you," he declared.

"But one minute," she hesitated. "I do not know where he has put it; it may be in the library." She stepped inside the room and turned on all the lights; then she moved nearer to the shelves and put her hands up to her face as though shocked. "Allah!" she cried. She ran from gap to gap where there had been a book, making cries of distress. "What is it?"

"Look! All the books that have been taken away!"

Arnika walked slowly round. "The police?"

"Yes, yes, the police must have seized them!"

He must have known perfectly well what books she was referring to but he was staring at the gaps in a dazed way when she slipped out of the room, downstairs, through the kitchen premises, across the yard and out of a small gate which the servants used, running up the bank and away towards Samatya like a young hart on the mountains of Bether.

2

The *Babushka* was a very old Russian woman, grandmother of many, who had been nurse to Tamara till she was seven and nurse to Jason till he went to school. Though serene and bright she was not, as Wordsworth rather too creamily put it, "lovely as a Lapland night." She had no teeth at all so that her chin and the tip of her nose were in constant danger of meeting. She lived in a hut at Büyükdere, about twelve miles up the Bosphorus from Istanbul on the European side. She earned the small amount of money on which she lived by doing needlework and mending for people who came to the villas during the summer.

Tamara arrived as the *Babushka* was having her breakfast, that is, dipping large pieces of bread in her coffee and conveying them to her mouth with much messy enjoyment. She treated Tamara as though she were still her charge aged seven.

"My lamb, my loved one," she cried in Russian, "what are you doing looking so tired and untidy at this time of day? Come, my precious and have some breakfast with your old *Babushka*!" She had the effect of making Tamara feel almost seven. She let the *Babushka* take her coat and hang it over the back of a chair, she let her bring water and a sponge to wash, she let her brush her hair and take off her shoes and all the time she was thinking hard.

"My child, your shoes are worn out; have you walked far?"

"Ran," Tamara said dreamily, "I ran, almost all the way into the old city. I seem to have been all night getting here, I could not find a *dolmus*, I have not slept at all."

"Then you shall sleep on my bed, my pretty one," the unquestioning one said calmly.

"No, no! There is much to be done, first I must get some more shoes, strong ones for walking."

The *Babushka* knew just where she could buy shoes and after breakfast took her out to find them.

"Now I am going up the hill." Tamara left her happily preparing a midday meal and walked up a well-worn track for some distance beyond the little town, up along the Bosphorus shore to a small Moslem shrine where a green crinkled paper effigy of a saint lies in a little chapel to which spinster Moslem women come, accompanied by their mothers or some relation, to pray at the *mihrab* for a husband.

The Bosphorus here is at its narrowest and swiftest and a road is being constructed to convey motorists to the bathing beaches on the Black Sea. Tamara shaded her eyes from the sun because she had not her dark glasses with her and stared across at the hills on the other side. Beyond those hills, some miles or so due East, would lie the plantation, according to Landrake's description. She had a set of keys for Landrake's launch which he had had made for her and given to her only a few days ago. If he was missing, he had told her, she was to look for him over there, and if she were in trouble she was to take the *Sylvia*, in which she might live if necessary. But it was safer, by far, to stay with the *Babushka*.

"Listen, *Babushka*," she said during the midday meal, "do you know of somebody from whom I could hire a car? I would pay them well; I have money with me."

"Tamara, my little one, I am uneasy for you; it is only I who know how naughty you can be, how wilful and strong-headed, if you had taken your *Babushka's* advice you would not have married Yenish Effendi but you were wild to do so. Now you are freed from the unhappiness you have endured with that most strange man, you cannot wait two weeks before you are anxious to plunge into I know not what wild exploit. Be restrained, my child."

"I promise you, *Babushka*, that in a world of men a little common sense is often absolutely necessary, a little less adventure and a little more practical thinking."

"You talk in parables; either tell me all or tell me nothing."

"I cannot tell you all because I do not wish you to know anything; it is better not . . . my dear old nanny-goat!" she added, laughing, in English, the words her mother used.

So, after a certain amount of negotiation and talk, the *Babushka* managed to get someone to bring a car around, an Oldsmobile tourer with a hood and horsehair upholstery, overstuffed like everything Turkish, bursting from its seams, and with an elaborate old-fashioned gate-change that required some effort to move at all. It also had a delightful bulb horn which, when squeezed, gave out a noise like a cow enduring stiff labour.

Tamara drove the twelve miles into Istanbul at great peril to herself and everyone else along the coast road, blowing the bulb horn at every sharp bend. By the time she had reached Pera and hurtled across Taxim Square she had got the hang of it. She moo-ed her way down the packed Istiklal Caddesi with people straggling all over the road, across the Galata Bridge and up the other side of the Golden Horn through the old city to the University, where she parked the vehicle and went to look for a Turkish friend, a professor of organic chemistry. She had to sit through the second half of a lecture on hydro carbons before she was able to speak to him but, when she did, he took her into his private room and gave her all his attention.

"Well, Tamara, as you should know, we import no proprietary brands of anything into this country; if you really want a named-variety of weed-killer you'll have to fly to Cyprus where you could, I feel sure, get it at Boots in Nicosia."

"There isn't time." She looked so charming, sitting there on the arm of his chair, her fabulous coat hanging loosely open, her ashen hair youthfully smooth and unwaved.

"I have not seen you since Torgüt's tragic death," her friend murmured, "I must offer my sympathy."

She bowed her head: "Thank you."

"I cannot but help wondering why you need a great quantity of weed-killer for your garden."

"It is not for the garden," Tamara said impatiently. "Listen, I have been left a widow with no great resources; as yet I do not know how I stand but I know I shall not be well off. Torgüt has a small property of four to six acres which I want to have cleared for . . . for profitable purposes."

The professor opened his eyes very wide and looked shocked: "But, my child, if you use this very strong chemical compound I have in mind, the land will not be fit to grow anything on for some time, five years at the very least!"

"That is of no importance; I wish, I wish to *build* on the land."

"Ah, I see. To develop it."

"Yes," Tamara nodded, relieved at having found a likely explanation. "A small house or so beside a bathing beach!"

"Enterprising woman. It is clear that we must develop our coast line as the Southern Coast of Spain is being developed; that way we shall bring tourists and prosperity to our country." The Turks are hot for Progress.

"Quite," Tamara said, swinging her foot, once more wearing the elegant but worn-out shoes in which she had left home.

Understanding that she was in no mood for dalliance, the professor gave her the name of a merchant from whom she would be able to buy a large quantity of the weed killer to be mixed by him from a prescription which he wrote out for her. She was to get it as for the professor, and the account would be sent to him at the University.

"If he makes any trouble you can tell him that I need this immediately for an agricultural experiment which I wish to demonstrate. But I do not think he will object because this is expensive stuff, Tamara."

"I am willing to pay for it."

"You will need a drumful and I have put the quantity you will require dissolved in water. Over a large area it is usually done mechanically."

"We shall have to do it by hand."

"It will take some time to do it by hand with a single watering can."

"We can have a dozen watering cans," Tamara said impatiently, "there is no shortage of labour."

"Very well, my dear, I trust you to know what you are about." He handed her the prescription and smiled down at her. "How is the firmament? Found anything exciting yet?"

"Everything in the firmament is exciting," she answered, folding the paper and putting it into her handbag. "Thank you for this; you don't know what a favour you have done me."

3

By the time she had obtained the drum which she got without any trouble but only after a long wait, had crossed the Bosphorus by car ferry to Uskudar and taken the road to the tiny Black Sea resort of Sile, the day was almost over. Landrake had described the plantation as somewhere along the coast between Sile and Zonguldak, an area with desolate stretches and few villages. The descriptions of its exact situation had been confined wholly to physical landmarks, a large rock formation, several miles of marsh, a primitive bridge over a small river, a turning away from the poor quality road down a sandy track for some miles, a spinney of bushes, and so on.

She realised that dark was falling and she would have to spend the night at Sile. She stopped at a small adequate hotel and started off at dawn the following morning. With the hood of the car down she felt in command of the situation. She found the landmarks and followed them uncertainly because the land was featureless and it was impossible to stop to ask someone the way to a place the name of which she did not know. Past the spinney of bushes the river which she had been following began to break up as Landrake had described but she followed steadily the obviously-used sandy track amongst the shrubs for what seemed a long time before she came to what appeared to be a small market gardening settlement or plantation. A little French car with a Turkish registration number was standing by the huts, so evidently, she gathered, she had arrived somewhere.

She jumped out; she did not need a second look at the crops that were growing to know that she had found the place. No one came out to meet her so she returned to the car and blew the absurd horn two or three times to announce her presence. An old woman tottered out of one of the huts and four younger ones, with a gaggle of children clinging to their skirts, and one or two older ones, staring, emerged but did not come nearer and seemed scared out of their wits.

Tamara went forward smiling, a non-Turkish characteristic but a disarming one. She asked where the men were and they waved vaguely towards the sea: "Over there . . ." She asked to whom the French car belonged and she was told that they did not know. "Someone" had come, the men had gone with him "over there." They did not seem to be getting on well so Tamara ingratiated herself to one of the children by taking him to her old hired car and allowing him to think that he was blowing the bulb horn himself. It was a great success; the other children ventured across to her and presently they were all taking turns at blowing the horn, with solemn little faces which showed they were entranced.

After an exhausting fifteen minutes or so of this, the women evidently decided that she was no bird of ill-omen and she ventured to bring her absurd array of plastic watering cans and her drum of white crystals and told them that her husband, Yenish bey, their landlord and employer, had instructed her, with his dying breath, to see that the plants they were growing for him were watered with this nourishment and fertiliser from the Western world.

They exclaimed and chattered amongst themselves at the news that their landlord and employer was dead but Tamara was in no mood to waste time. They must start at once, she said, and to demonstrate that she intended to work herself she brought out the clumsy shoes she and *Babushka* had bought the previous day, and put them on.

It was now a full two weeks, she said, since her husband's death; the new moon had swelled like a pregnant woman, the watering with the new fertiliser must be done before the moon reached the full tomorrow, in this way they received the greatest benefit. They must start immediately.

The women had gradually loosened up and before long they were chattering away so fast that Tamara did not grasp more than half of what they were saying. She went with them, however, agreeing that they were under-nourished to the point of starvation but promising that once the plants had been watered with this miraculous substance all their troubles would be over (as, indeed, they would). There would be food for all, and plenty of it.

"We will start at once," she declared energetically but with failing heart as she surveyed the area which had to be treated. "We will not use water from the well but from this small stream . . ."

They got the idea pretty rapidly. It was so long since anything had happened in their monotonous lives that this new event was something to be experienced to the full.

Tamara threw her sable coat into the back of the car, tucked her handbag down beside the driving seat, peeled off her woollen sweater and rolled up the sleeves of her blouse.

"Now we start . . ."

The children, or rather the largest of them, came in useful as links in a human chain from the stream to the crops and, as each gaudy bucket arrived slopping water so that it was only three-quarters full, Tamara ladled in a not very accurate measure of white crystals from an empty bean can which she found lying around. Fortunately it was early enough in the year for the sun not to warm up too uncomfortably and by midday every plant in about two acres had had its dose.

In the meantime, the old mother had been preparing a brew of fish and rice in a large pan and Tamara realised with a jerk of fear, that the men were expected home.

"We'll cross our bridges when we come to them," she said aloud in English to give herself courage; it was something which her mother had often said and, though Tamara did not realise it, she gave the remark a particularly Mossop intonation.

"Let us start to eat before the men come home," she suggested but this was treated with the contempt which such a suggestion deserved. They worked on and at last she saw them, approaching from a distance, five of them, one old man and four younger men. They were bareheaded and their clothes were particularly ragged and dirty but what frightened her was the expressions on their faces. The women ran towards them and spoke rapidly, telling them what had happened whilst they were away and they hurried forward and surrounded Tamara whilst the children stood about and stared open-mouthed.

She told her story again but she could feel their anger and hostility and she stammered and sounded a great deal less confident than the first time. They said that no one had told them Yenish bey was dead and Tamara said she regretted but that it had happened barely two weeks ago. She herself had come with his last message as soon as she had been able to obtain the material he had required her to bring.

The overseer, they said, had told them nothing about Yenish bey dying. Had they then seen Arnika? They denied this hurriedly and emphatically; no one had been near them for weeks; much money was owing to them in wages. Tamara assured them that they would be paid in full; when a man of means died, she said, it was some little time before his money-matters were straightened out but all would be well, Yenish bey's widow would, it was hoped, be able to honour his debts.

They may or may not have believed this; but they were certainly very upset about something; they moved out of earshot and quarrelled and argued amongst themselves whilst the women stood nearby shooting almost ashamed looks at Tamara, with whom they had been getting along splendidly.

Presently the old woman made it clear that her meal would no longer wait; the women beckoned to Tamara and they all filed into one of the huts where a low table held the shallow giant pan, like a jam pan, in which the food had been cooked and everyone squatted down and started to help themselves, Bedouin fashion, with the right hand. No one spoke during the meal, Tamara made the movements of eating that everyone else made but did not, in fact, take much food. Afterwards water for washing her hands was brought by one of the children, a rather pathetic and endearing attempt at being the formal hosts.

When the meal was over, everyone rose, Tamara thanking the old man formally for his hospitality, and once again the men went into conference. The women set to work as they had worked before the men returned and soon they were joined, sheepishly but reluctantly, by the five men and presently the labour was going with a swing. As she worked, Tamara worried; should she give them money, of which she had a certain amount in her handbag? Or should she go without doing so? She had a frightened feeling that if she were to start distributing it they might, in their greed, attack her and rob her of everything, if not kill her in their frustration. But on the other hand, they were pretty destitute and their wages, it seemed, were certainly owing to them. She began to realise how important the money of which they had been cheated by Jason must have been to Torgüt and his accomplices. As they worked they seemed amenable enough but Tamara felt an under-current of violence and resentment; she wished she had her handbag, and the revolver, nearer but how could she work with it hanging from her arm.

And all the time the small French car stood, unexplained and unattended; it had been left in the shade of a large bush but the sun had moved round and it now stood in full sunshine. The faces of the men were so sullen that Tamara felt anything could spark off their temper and a false step could start a lynching. She also got the feeling that they were as conscious of the little car as Tamara herself: it seemed to stand there in silent reproach.

She was getting very tired; her hair, dampened with sweat, was straggling over her face; she took off the silk scarf she wore under her blouse collar and tied it round her head, peasant wise; they watched her every movement. A worm of panic stirred inside her; if they killed her they could bury her and no one would ever find her body. But why should they kill her? Yet she was sure they were killers, outlaws and ruffians; if she gave them the smallest reason to kill her, they would do so. Her handbag was reason enough. In the course of the work they were closing in, it was almost finished. Tamara looked closely at the shoots that had been processed earlier in the day for signs of wilting and she could have given a shout of joy: amongst the first to have been treated there was a slight, a very slight curling up of the edge of the leaves. Thank heaven the process was not too quick, otherwise the main crop would be dead before she had made her departure, if, indeed, she was ever able to do so.

The quantity she had been given was working out almost exactly right, the drum was nearly empty by the time she had taken out the last tinful; she poured out the remainder of the white crystals on the soil and ground it in with her heel. The old man came up at once and remonstrated with her.

"Why did you do that?"

"The little ones," she returned, glibly, "the children might get hold of it, it could upset them." With a stick she scratched the fragments into the ground. "It is better to keep such things away from them. Behold, all is now completed before the full moon, and much good fortune will come your way. The stars in their courses will attend the good fortune . . ." and talking in this abstruse way she managed to back towards the huts. The children saved her, seeing that the lady was going they clustered round her begging to be allowed to blow the horn again; they jumped and danced around, chattering and making much noise, like a lot of small excited terriers. They almost dragged her to the car and, goodnaturedly she let them scramble over her as she sat in the driving seat, and make unearthly noises on the bulb horn whilst she pulled her jersey over her knees and, under the cover of it, extracted the revolver from her handbag, holding it firmly in her right hand and helping the children with the horn with her other hand.

She looked across them, laughing, at the sullen line of faces; her laughter was partly to show how much she was enjoying their dear little offsprings but mostly relief at having the gun in her hand.

"I go now," she cried happily, "but I shall return almost at once with money which is owing to you. It may not be all of it but I shall bring what I can obtain. And I thank you, one and all, for the work we have done to-day. The sun is now sinking in the heavens and I must go before dark falls lest I lose my way back to the main road. Farewell!"

Charmingly she raised a hand, rather less charmingly she heaved the lousy mass of child off her knee, out of the car and on to the ground whilst at the same time starting up the engine and getting into reverse gear, not an easy matter with the abominable upstanding gate-change. She did it, however, starting with such a jerk that one of the children was nearly run over. A look of astonishment crossed the faces in front of her and one of the young men ran forward, but Tamara was taking no chances; holding the steering wheel with her left hand and backing across the wide approach which she knew was clear behind her, she fired the gun with her right hand, into the air.

It would have been so much easier if she had thought of leaving the car in the going-away position when she arrived; as it was she managed all right, but clumsily; when she had backed far enough there was a nerve-racking small struggle with the gear lever, a long, long second before the car lurched forward. Over the hard ground near the huts the car moved rapidly but at the start of the sandy track it slowed down; she had gone several hundred yards before, looking back, she saw another of the men running hard to catch up with her; he was waving and shouting at her to stop. Wonderfully in control of the situation she stopped, and stood up, pointing the gun at him. "What do you want?"

It was a rhetorical question, requiring no answer; she could see from his face that rape, murder and lynching only would have satisfied his wants. Boldly she fired the revolver again, missing him deliberately but not by so many feet. With a cry of terror the ragged rascal turned and ran back and with her heart beating in her throat Tamara pressed down the not very responsive accelerator as far as it would go, the wheels whizzed round ineffectively for a few moments spraying sand, but miraculously took grip and the car moved quite fast, up the lane and away.

4

Early in the morning, after Nuri bey had spent an unhappy night in his own house, Landrake called for him and they went down to the little harbour where the *Sylvia* was moored, satisfying themselves that everything was untouched and Tamara was not there. Then they went systematically all over Istanbul and Pera, to the *Hammam*, to the houses of a number of mutual friends, to her bank, to the restaurants and bars to which she sometimes went, to her hairdresser in the Istiklal Caddesi and finally after sunset they returned to the villa and smashed open the door of the observatory.

"We are absolutely defeated," Nuri bey declared. He had no hope left; too many women had disappeared in that old Imperial city, the Bosphorus was too easy a place in which to dispose of them; it never regurgitated its diet of corpses, or hardly ever.

Arnika had won.

Nuri bey sat in a deep chair in Torgüt Yenish's library, slumped and expressionless, his arms lying along the chair arms while Landrake did something more practical. Leaping into his small car, still hot from the chase round and round the city, he drove to the airport and checked with his watcher there that Arnika had certainly not returned. It was only as he drove back from Yesilkoy that he was struck with an idea, one which he despised himself for not having had before. He went to Sirkici, the station at which the trains arrive from the West and found that the Orient Express was timed to pick up passengers at Belgrade to arrive in Istanbul in the late evening. He then went to the airline offices and discovered that a plane from London had arrived in Belgrade the previous day at a time which would allow a passenger to get on to the Express for Istanbul. Though this was no good news he felt that it was something to go on and rushed back with the information to Nuri bey who was sitting exactly as he had left him, dull-eyed and haggard.

"There is no one so rootless as Arnika: he lives nowhere that I can discover, he has no friends, nothing by which one may trace him, he is a clever man who has managed to conceal any private life he may have successfully. There is only one hope of a place where he is likely to be sooner or later. It's not very helpful but he is sure to turn up sometime at the plantation where the damned stuff is grown, and that is hardly a place at all."

Nuri bey shook his head. "He is *Sheytan* himself; when he is there he is relentlessly there, as I know from the way he stuck to me in Oxford, but when he is not there . . . he is so utterly gone that you feel frantic in the knowledge that you have no idea where he is. I have had that feeling often; I know it from unhappy experience, my friend."

Landrake stamped up and down the room. "There isn't even a drink in this house. Look, Nuri bey, we can't just sit around waiting for something to happen, something to turn up . . ." Nuri bey shuddered. "Yes, Nuri, he may have killed Tamara and have disposed of her body by now, we've got to face it. If he has, what is the next thing he will do? He will have to go to his headquarters, that seems to me obvious. He's got these raggle-taggle ruffians out there all depending on him; yes, Nuri, he'll *have* to go out there, sooner or later. Let us go out there and wait for him to arrive."

Nuri bey smiled grimly. "You are enjoying this, Landrake, my friend. You are like a happy schoolboy. You have a dangerous job to do and there is nothing you like better. I, I am not so. Tamara is the only life I wish for now; I have lived many years without her but that has changed, now I cannot live at all without her."

"Then if that is so, why not come with me, since your life is no longer of value?"

There was a long silence, Nuri bey said nothing.

"I know just how you're feeling, in spite of your insults about schoolboys, Nuri bey my friend. The girl I told you about . . ."

Nuri bey raised his worn face. "The girl who died of drugs?"

"Yes. She was my wife. So, you see, I do hazard a guess as to how you feel; I too know what it means not to have any more interest in living, without one particular person."

Nuri bey unwrapped himself and stood up. "At least we shall be doing something. I shall go with you to help to lay your gelignite, dear friend. Then I shall lead your Armenian peasants out of danger while you blow the place to the sky. Let us, at least, destroy the opium and with it a few pounds of heroin jam!" He gave such a wild bitter laugh that Landrake thought his stricken friend unbalanced.

It was impossible to start before dawn, so Landrake spent a few hours of uneasy sleep in another chair in Yenish's library and Nuri bey continued to sit in the arm-chair he had already occupied and stared at the point in the room at which Yenish had died, hoping that he would have an attack of extra-sensory perception and actually "see" what had happened when Yenish was killed. But, as always, he could not will himself into the state which invariably came upon him without prompting.

When the night became at odds with the morning he rose stiffly and went out through the long window on to the balcony; the early mist which always shrouded the Bosphorus was lifting and from the Sea of Marmara there emerged the four lovely Princes' Isles to which Byzantine Emperors would send their rivals, first blinded with hot irons, for lifelong exile; these were now suburbs of Istanbul from which city breadwinners travelled every morning to work in thirty-five-year-old boats. He went up on to the roof and looked into Tamara's observatory which still smelled slightly of her exotic French scent. He touched lovingly her things, her telescope, her terrestial globe, the well-worn leather top of the stool on which she sat. He bent low and examined the hieroglyphics which she had scribbled on her pad. He picked up her pencil from the floor. At a shout from Landrake below he hastily secured the door, replacing the wood which they had bashed away from the outward-opening door, as well as he was able.

"I come," he shouted.

On the way to the boat they bought bread and butter, fruit and eggs; there was some delay, too, about fuel, taking the outboard engine for the dinghy and tying the dinghy astern, but presently they were off, progressing steadily along the right bank. They were quiet, taking it in turn to steer and Landrake negotiating what he called "the choppy bit into the Euxine."

"I shall take the dinghy and all the explosive up the river as the sun sets; and I hope you will stay with the boat until my return; it is better that only one of us go." Nuri bey fiercely disagreed but Landrake pointed out that Nuri bey was not a practical man and furthermore, one lone man would be less conspicuous than two. Towards sunset they came to the desolate place and Landrake moved his boxes of gelignite and his fuses into the dinghy.

"I've got my gun, and you've got yours so we're all set. There's just one thing before I go . . . *I* shot Yenish."

Nuri bey said nothing, he sagged a little more inside his brown pin-striped suit.

"Sooner or later I would have done it deliberately so I'm not excusing myself when I say he started it. It was all so quick; you left us and I was following you when he called me back; he said he hoped I would give you no inkling of what *he* knew *I* knew; he thought your reluctance to go to England arose from the fact that I had already told you that Yenish's side-line was drug-growing and marketing and the whole thing was drug-slanted. I said it was only fair to you to tell you, since Yenish himself had got his son involved in the filthy trade. At that he got his revolver out of his desk drawer . . . but I had mine ready as he looked up and somehow or other *mine* went off!"

There was a pause. "No, I won't even say 'somehow or other,' I'll have the courage to say I bloody well fired it; not once or twice; I made a job of it. I've had to shoot men in war, whom I was told were 'the enemy,' men I didn't know a thing about, as innocent as myself. Well, Yenish was the World's enemy and he's a lot better dead and I'm an assassin, not a murderer, because I didn't do it for personal reasons. Maybe I'm a fascist, a fanatic and any other thing beginning with f you like to mention and it might be a good job if I didn't come back safely from this expedition; I'm just telling you, old Nuri, so you won't be too upset if I don't. *And*, of course, because Tamara didn't do it; I saved her from that!"

Nuri bey said absolutely nothing at all; he could find no suitable words, nothing that was not banal. Wordless, he helped his friend climb into the dinghy and watched him start it after half a dozen abortive pulls. Landrake made the thumbs-up sign as he sped away and shouted something which Nuri bey did not catch.

"What?" he yelled.

". . . there'll be a big bang, if it's only ME!" he heard.

And as the sun set, the rim of a fantastic moon appeared above the edge of the world and Nuri bey gave a shout of alarm. To do what he had to do by moonlight! Landrake acted with the inconsequential, light-hearted but deadly impulsiveness of the Hannah Benson girl; it terrified him.

He sat on the pilot's stool, rocking with the boat, watching the moon become smaller as it rose, but at no time was it less than bright. His eyes constantly sought the salt marshes along which Landrake had disappeared and from time to time he glanced at the chronometer which was Landrake's pride.

He wrapped himself in a travelling rug because it became very cold. Two hours passed, fifteen minutes, five minutes and he was startled violently by an explosion of giant proportions which resounded round him as though the sky were a huge plastic dome and he alone in it like a small piece of cheese in a very large cheese dish.

Shortly after he thought he heard the sound of a bell. A mist was forming and he hoped it would not be a bad one lest Landrake lose his way back to the *Sylvia.* The sound of the bell seemed to be coming closer; it was indescribably eerie and the extreme coldness he felt caused his teeth to chatter. The sound came nearer and nearer; he started up the engine and went slowly towards the rivermouth, as near inland as he dared go when he saw something approaching, floating towards him on the current, a curiously athwart, oblique object from which sounded, jerkily and uneven, the awful irregular tolling of the bell. He stopped the engine, looking and listening acutely; it appeared to be something in a boat, some cross-shaped object that caused the boat to loll sideways because it was ill-balanced. It was not exactly coming nearer now but drifting past; he restarted the engine and approached more closely as it bobbed and bowed with the tide.

What he thought he saw was too mad, too fantastic to be believed, he was out of his mind, he was having one of his flights into a sixth sense. The mast of the small dilapidated, partly water-logged fishing boat formed the upright of a crude cross and on it hung a naked man.

Gently he edged the *Sylvia* nearer; the moonlight was as bright as the palest sunshine but had the effect of making everything look unreal. He snatched up Landrake's powerful binoculars and focused them on the figure; the head was lolling to one side with the boat but he had seen that figure far too often to mistake it. The feet, hanging pathetically down, unsupported, were turned inwards one to the other, like the feet of a swan on land. At the mast-head hung the bell; there was no rudder or tiller, the barque drifted aimlessly.

Though Nuri bey had never seen the sight, it was one which others before him had seen in the Black Sea, a traditional but obsolete form of dealing with an enemy.

Then (oh! blessed normality) he heard the tiny sound, a mere ticking, of Landrake's returning outboard motor getting louder as it came nearer. He wished he knew how to send a rocket up in welcome; at last he saw the dinghy emerging through the mist and heard Landrake's hoarse shout of excitement, as he came up alongside.

"Recognise him? It's Arnika! He's still keeping at your heels . . ."

"Great Allah! Cannot we sink that terrible sight?" But there was relief in Nuri bey's voice that, at least, one other had shared the experience, it was not supernatural.

"It can't stay afloat much longer, it's half full of water."

Nuri bey leaned forward and shouted. "Sink it, for the love of Allah!"

Landrake held up a single container of gelignite: "I was going to blow it up, I found it on my way there; it was nearly grounded on some sand but I pulled it off because I thought you'd like to see it."

"Get it out of sight."

Landrake's boatmanship was neat and assured. He did the job quickly and returned to the *Sylvia*.

"Now let's move," he said after he had secured the dinghy and got himself a glass of whisky. But Nuri bey's eyes would not leave the death barque nor could his ears hear anything but that dreadful stammering, crippled sound of the bell. Landrake took the pilot's stool and started the engine, they did a wide circle round and in a few minutes there was a relatively small explosion and the sound of the bell ceased. Dark pieces floated on the surface but soon sank and there was nothing left.

Landrake and Nuri bey stared at one another; two pale faces under a pale moon.

They put in at Sile and slept in the *Sylvia* long and late into the morning; later still, haggard-eyed, they faced one another across a table in a Büyükdere restaurant, knowing that delicious red mullet was being cooked for them. There was a bottle of native raki on the table, colourless but opaque when water was added, which Landrake was sipping with satisfaction.

"So it was neither the Thames nor the Bosphorus, but the Black Sea!" Nuri bey murmured.

"Are you in a state to listen, my friend?"

"I do not know."

"Let me tell you, I did not need to blow up any crops; it had all been destroyed by some weed-killer or other; the opium was lying flat and blackened, the whole lot; the place was deserted. The eagles, if one can call the poor devils that, are gone. Whether the police have got them or whether they have just scarpered I don't know. I used all of the gelignite but the little I brought back, blowing up the press; it really went for six."

"How did they kill Arnika?"

"I'm not sure. It's an old Caucasian method of disposal, isn't it, hanging, crucifying and then pushing out to sea in an old barque? I had a good close look and there was certainly something wrong with the throat; as there wasn't a tree within miles, I'd say it was a good old-fashioned garrotting like the highway robbers used to do in my country. That's the sort of thing that happens when you don't have trade unions, ha ha!"

Nuri bey gave him a long stern look: "I could join in your amusement if I knew that Tamara was safe."

"No wonder poor old Arnika was mad to get the money for the stuff that Jason walked off with. He was on his own with a bunch of half-starved ruffians waiting for his blood. Labour troubles! Obsessed by Progress though you are in your country, you've had Autocracy for so long that Democracy doesn't come easy, does it? It is but a tenuous and wispy thing hereabouts."

"There's Tamara, she's coming here!" Nuri bey jumped up and ran with long strides out of the restaurant where, in front of the windows and in full view of the diners, he slipped his hands inside her fur coat and wrapped her in his arms and kissed her passionately. She clung to him, crying and saying over and over again: "Thank goodness you're safe!"

The *Babushka* stood a little way off, her hands thrust into her sleeves, eyes lowered, ashamed.

"I saw the *Sylvia* tied up over there by the quay so I came to look for you; Nuri, Nuri, I can never thank you enough. Tell me, will Jason . . .?"

"I have very, very much to tell you, my lovely one," Nuri bey interrupted soberly.

They took the *Babushka* with them and went back to the table, where Tamara sat weeping, and the *Babushka*, with hands still hidden in her sleeves, sat with lowered head, unaccustomed to sit at table with the Pashas Effendi.

"Arnika is dead," Nuri bey said gently, "his was a dreadful end; I cannot say he was gathered into the arms of Allah; nor did he take anything with him, there was nothing in his two dead hands."

"We didn't kill him," Landrake said a trifle smugly.

"Luckily," Nuri bey added swiftly. "Since one should speak well of the dead I can safely say he had the patience of a saint."

"There, there, my linden flower," the *Babushka* put out an incredibly gnarled hand and touched Tamara's arm. "It is reaction, my pashas, Tamara has been waging a private war of her own; and now it is over she must weep herself dry."

"You are wearing a very strange pair of shoes, Tamara," Landrake said sternly, "beetle-squashers I would call them."

She started to laugh a little. Landrake passed her a small glass of raki. "Drink this, my dear."

"What have you been doing?"

Tamara sipped her raki. "Cleaning up," she said half-laughing, half-crying, "cleaning up everything that could destroy Torgüt's reputation as a respectable citizen."

"Why bother?" Landrake said thoughtlessly.

"Because he was my late husband and Jason's father."

Landrake acknowledged this by raising his glass. "To you, Tamara, my dear, and to your future happiness with Nuri. All is said and done; no flashbacks, please. Here comes my red mullet and I don't want my appetite spoiled."

Ten days later there was a letter from Hannah:

> *Darling Nuri bey,*
> The local paper is coming under separate cover; as you will see the Inquest was an easy walk-over. I sat in the public gallery and heard everything. Aunt Maisie carried the day, in floods of

tears she told that Ronda was a drug addict and it all started with slimming tablets when she was about fourteen. She went on to say how she had never been able to do anything with her and how the girl had *often threatened suicide*; she made a frightfully good impression.

Jason was perfect; his manner was just right, he didn't shoot any sort of line but gave his evidence quietly and sadly. He said she depended utterly on him, he couldn't bring himself to hand her over to the police. He said that perhaps what he had done was criminal but anyone else in his position would have done the same. He said she was pathetic and called her "one of the world's unwanted," and I think that did it; it was the "who would kick out a starving kitten" image. Asked if he thought the girl took her own life he said kind of temperately that one could never be sure about anything. Pressed further he said that if she did it herself it was because she knew she was being a burden on him and possibly worried about his career, though she had not in fact ever said anything.

So it was "Suicide whilst the balance of her mind was disturbed" and the Coroner added that the intention to suicide was clear though there was some little doubt as to how the death actually took place.

So the Ronda part of it was okay but as soon as Jason appeared back in college he got one hell of a rocket and it looked as though he was going to be sent down but that's where I stepped in. I had to get Harp to help me dig up the dope because I couldn't go into Larimer garden alone with my zip bag and plunge into the shrubbery, however much I wanted to. When it came to the point I realised that it was too serious to indulge in a spot of Dean-baiting. So I got Harp to help. It was simply teeming with rain when we went and there wasn't a soul around; we rooted about but not for long; it was an inch or two below the soil exactly where you said, you old duck! Harp and I decided it was far too serious a thing to keep to ourselves so I took the whole bang lot straight to the Warden, and I got it to Himself without telling the secretary what my business was, though she was dying to know.

I said it was *madly urgent and private*, and when I got into the Holy of Holies I told the old man everything. I mean everything about Jason and the trick with the Customs and the lot. Well, the top brass hauled Jason up and grilled him for hours and he emerged, my dear, chastened and sober but reinstated for another year! Four loud cheers!

I'm sure I shall see you before long, and I hope to see his mother too; he's got her photograph in his room and she looks a smasher. I shall come home with him for this coming long vac., at least I think I will. At the moment, however, he is pretty livid with me; we're not on speakers.

With love from Hannah

"Can it be, can it be," Nuri bey asked with great shining eyes, "that it is, when 'all is said and done,' a *woman's* world?"

About the Author

Joan Fleming (1908–1980) was a British author of more than thirty crime and thriller novels. She was born in Lancashire, England, and educated at the City Literary Institute and the University of Lausanne in Switzerland. The British Crime Writers' Association twice awarded her with its prestigious Gold Dagger award for best crime novel of the year, once in 1962 for *When I Grow Rich*, and again in 1970 for *Young Man, I Think You're Dying.*

About the Author

[illegible]